THE MISSIONARY: AN INDIAN TALE (VOLUME III)

First published 1811
This edition published by Lector House in 2024

ISBN: 978-93-6138-133-1

Lector House LLP
Registered Office: H. No. 96, Block C, Tomar Colony,
Burari, Delhi – 110084, India
info@lectorhouse.com
www.lectorhouse.com

THE MISSIONARY: AN INDIAN TALE (VOLUME III)

LADY SYDNEY MORGAN (MISS OWENSON)

2024

LECTOR HOUSE LLP

THE MISSIONARY: AN INDIAN TALE (VOLUME III)

BY

MISS OWENSON

WITH A PORTRAIT OF THE AUTHOR

IN THREE VOLUMES,
VOL. III.

FOURTH EDITION

Contents

Page

VOLUME III.

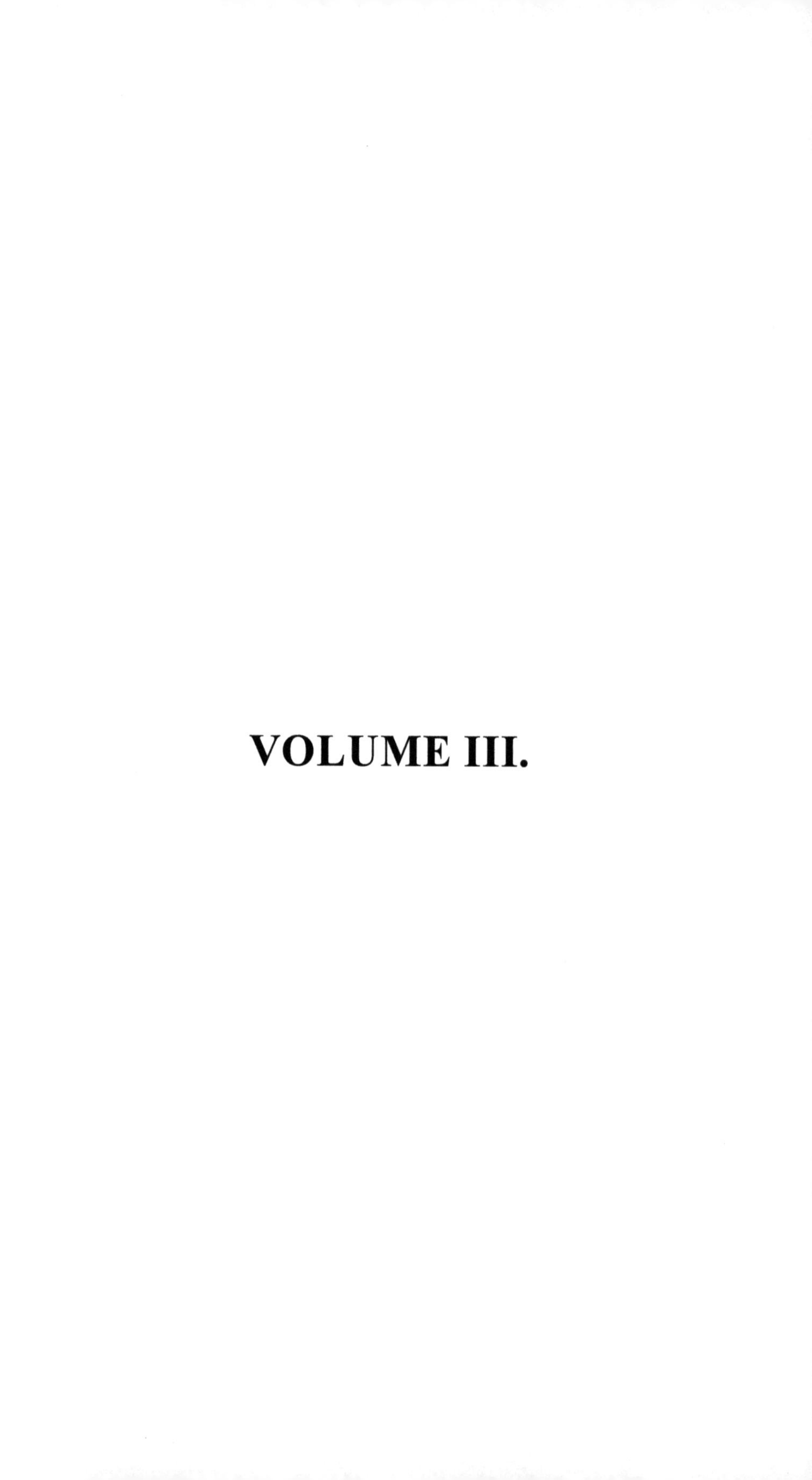

VOLUME III.

Chapter XIII.

ON the second day of their wandering, the deep shade of the forest scenery, in which they had hitherto been involved, softened into a less impervious gloom, the heights of the black rock of Bembhar rose on their view, and the lovely and enchanting glen which reposes at its northern base, and which is called the Valley of Floating Islands, burst upon their glance. These phenomena, which appear on the bosom of the Behat, are formed by the masses of rock, by the trees and shrubs which the whirlwind tears from the summits of the surrounding mountains, and which are thus borne away by the fury of the torrents, and plunged into the tranquil waters beneath; these rude fragments, collected by time and chance, cemented by the river Slime, and intermixed by creeping plants, and parasite grasses, become small but lovely islets, covered with flowers, sowed by the vagrant winds, and skirted by the leaves and blossoms of the crimson lotos, the water-loving flower of Indian groves. This scene, so luxuriant and yet so animating, where all was light, and harmony, and odour, gave a new sensation to the nerves, and a new tone to the feelings of the wanderers, and their spirits were fed with balmier airs, and their eyes greeted with lovelier objects, than hope or fancy had ever imaged to their minds.—Sometimes they stood together on the edge of the silvery flood, watching the motion of the arbours which floated on its bosom, or pursuing the twinings of the harmless green serpent, which, shining amidst masses of kindred hues, raised gracefully his brilliant crest above the edges of the river bank. Sometimes from beneath the shade of umbrageous trees, they beheld the sacred animal of India breaking the stubborn flood with his broad white breast, and gaining the fragrant islet, where he reposed his heated limbs; his mild countenance shaded by his crooked horns, crowned by the foliage in which he had entangled them; thus reposing in tranquil majesty, he looked like some river-deity of antient fable.

Flights of many-coloured perroquets, of lorys, and of peacocks, reflected on the bosom of the river the bright and various tints of their splendid plumage; while the cozel, the nightingale of Hindoo bards, poured its song of love from the summit of the loftiest *mergosa*, the eastern lilac. It was here they found the *Jama*, or rose apple-tree, bearing ambrosial fruit—it was here that the sweet sumbal, the spikenard of the antients, spread its tresses of dusky gold over the clumps of granite, which sparkled like coloured gems amidst the saphire of the mossy soil—it was here that, at the decline of a lovely day, the wanderers reached the shade of a natural arbour, formed by the union of a tamarind-tree with the branches of a *covidara*, whose purple and rose-coloured blossoms mingled with the golden fruit which, to the Indian palate, affords so delicious a refreshment.

It was Luxima who discovered this retreat so luxurious, and yet so simple. The purity of the atmosphere, the brilliancy of the scene, had given to her spirits a higher tone than usually distinguished their languid character. Looking pure and light as the air she breathed, she had bounded on before her companion, who, buried in profound reverie, seemed at once more thoughtful and more tender than he had yet appeared in look or manner. When he reached the arbour, he found Luxima seated beneath its shade—her brow crowned with Indian feathers, and her delicate fingers engaged in forming a wreath of odoriferous berries; looking like the emblem of that lovely region, whose mild and delicious climate had contributed to form the beauty of her person, the softness of her character, and the ardour of her imagination. No thought of future care contracted her brow, and the smile of peace and innocence sat on her lips. Not so the Missionary: the morbid habit of watching his own sensations had produced in him an hypochondriasm of conscience, which embittered the most blameless moments of his life; his diseased mind discovered a lurking crime in the most innocent enjoyments; and the fear of offending Heaven, fastened his attention to objects which were only dangerous, by not being immediately dismissed from his thoughts. The moral economy of his nature suffered from the very means he took to preserve it; and his danger arose less from his temptation, than from the sensibility with which he watched its progress, and the efforts he made to combat and to resist its influence. He now beheld Luxima more lovely than he had ever seen her; she was gracefully occupied, and there was something picturesque, something almost *fantastic*, in her appearance, which gave the poignant charm of novelty to her air and person. She was murmuring an Indian song, as he approached her. The Missionary stood gazing on her for some moments in silence, then suddenly averting his eyes, and seating himself near her, he said—"And to what purpose, my dearest daughter, dost thou so industriously weave those fragrant wreaths?"

"To hang upon the bower of thy repose," she replied, "as a spell against evil;—for dost thou not, on every side, perceive the *bacula* plant, so injurious to the nerves, and whose baneful influence the odour of these berries can alone dispel?"[1]

"Alas!" he exclaimed, "in scenes so lovely and remote as those in which we now wander, who could suspect that latent evil lurked? But the evil which always exists, and that against which it is most difficult to guard, exists within ourselves, Luxima."

"Thou sayest it," returned Luxima, "and therefore must it be true; and yet, methinks, in us at least no evil can exist—look around thee, Father; behold those hills which encompass us on every side, and which, seeming to shut out the universe, exclude all the evil passions by which it is agitated and disordered; and since absent from all human intercourse, our feelings relate only to each other, surely in us at least no evil *can* exist."

"Let us hope, let us trust there does not, Luxima," said the Missionary, in strong emotion; "and oh! my daughter, let us watch and pray that there *may not*."

"And here," said Luxima with simplicity, and suspending her work, "where all breathes of peace and innocence, against what are we to pray?"

[1] The odour of this flower produces violent head-aches.

"Even against *those thoughts* which involuntarily start into the mind, and which, though confined, and perhaps referring exclusively to each other, may yet become fatal and seductive, may yet plunge us into error beyond the mercy of Heaven to forgive!"

"But if one *sole* thought occupies the existence!" said Luxima, tenderly and with energy, "and if it is sanctified by the perfection of its object!"

"But to what earthly object does perfection belong, Luxima?"

"To thee;" replied the Neophyte, blushing.

"It is the ardour of thy gratitude only," said the Missionary with vehemence, "which bestows on me, an epithet belonging alone to Heaven. And lovely as is this purest of human sentiments, yet, *being human*, it is liable to corruption, and may be carried to an excess fatal to us both; for, oh! Luxima, were I to avail myself of this excess of gratitude, this pure but unguarded tenderness, and in wilds solitary and luxuriant as these, where happiness and security might mingle, where, forgetting the world, and its opinions, abandoning alike *heaven* and its *cause*!"—he paused abruptly—he trembled, and a deep groan burst from a heart, agitated by all the conflicting emotions of a sensitive conscience, and an imperious passion.

Luxima, moved by his agitation—tender, timid, yet always happy and tranquilly blessed in the presence of him, the idol of her secret thoughts, and fearing only those incidents which might impede the innocent felicity of being near him—endeavoured to soothe his perturbation, and, taking his hand in hers, and bending her head towards him, she looked on his eyes with innocent fondness, and her sighs, sweet as the incense of the evening, breathed on his burning cheek! Then the sacred fillet of religion fell from his eyes; he threw himself at her feet, and pressing her hands to his heart, he said passionately—"Luxima, tell me, dost thou not belong exclusively to Heaven? Recall to my wandering mind that sacred vow, by which I solemnly devoted thee to its service, at the baptismal font! Oh! my daughter, thou wouldst not destroy me? thou wouldst not arm Heaven against me, Luxima?"

"I!" returned Luxima tenderly, "I destroy thee, who art dear to me as heaven itself!"

"Oh! Luxima," he exclaimed in emotion, "look not thus on me! tell me not that I am dear to thee, or...." At that moment his rosary fell to the earth, and lay at the feet of the Indian.

An incident so natural and so simple struck on the conscience of the Missionary, as though the Minister of Divine wrath had blasted his gaze with his accusing presence;—he grew pale and shuddered, his arms fell back upon his breast;—overpowered by shame, and by self-abhorrence, rushing from the bower, he plunged into the thickest shade of the grove; there he threw himself on the earth; and that mind, once so high and lofty in its own conscious triumph, was now again sunk and agonized by the conviction of its own debasement. From this state of unsupportable humiliation, he was awakened by the sound of horses' feet; he raised his eyes, and beheld approaching an Indian, who led a small Arabian horse, laden with empty panniers: the Missionary hastily arose—and the stranger, moved by the dignity of his form, and the disorder of his pale and haggard countenance, gave him the *Salaam*; and invited him, with the hospitable courtesy of his country, to repair to his cottage, which lay at a little distance,—"Or perhaps," he said, "you wish to overtake the caravan, and—"

"To *overtake* it!" interrupted the Missionary; "has it then long passed?"

"It halts now," returned the peasant; "on the other side of *Bembhar*, I have been disposing of some *touz*[2] to a merchant of Tatta; if you have no other mode of proceeding, you will scarcely overtake it on foot."

A new cause of suffering now occupied his mind.—Luxima, hitherto cheered and supported by the lovely and enlivening scenes through which she passed, by the smoothness of her path and the temperature of her native climes, was yet wearied and exhausted by a journey performed in a manner to which the delicacy of her frame was little adequate—but it was now

[2] Une laine, ou plutôt un poil, qu'on nomme *touz*, se prend sur les poitrines des chèvres sauvages des montagnes de Cashmire.—*Bernier.*

It is of this wool the Cashmirian shawls are formed.

impossible she could proceed as she had hitherto done; in a few hours the Eden which had cheated fatigue of its influence, would disappear from their eyes; and, should the caravan have proceeded much in advance, it was impossible that the delicate Indian could encounter the horrors of the desart which lay on the southern side of Bembhar.

It was then that, believing Providence had sent the Indian in his path, a new hope revived in his heart, a new resource was opened in his mind:—he offered a part of what remained of the purse of rupees he had brought with him from Lahore, for the Arabian horse. It was more than its value, and the Indian gladly accepted his proposal, and, pointing out to him the shortest way to *Bembhar*, and offering his good wishes for the safety of his journey, he pursued his way to his cottage. As soon as he had disappeared, Hilarion led the animal to the bower, where Luxima still remained, involved in reveries so soft, and yet so profound, that she observed not the approach of him who was their sole and exclusive object.

"Luxima!" he said in a low and tremulous voice—Luxima started, and, covered with blushes, she raised her languid eyes to his, and faintly answered—"*Father!*"

"My daughter," he said, "that Heaven, of whose favour I at least am so unworthy, has mercifully extended its providential care to us. A stranger, whom I met in the forest, has informed me, that the caravan has passed the rock of Bembhar; but I have purchased from him this animal, by which thou wilt be able to proceed!"

Luxima arose, and, drawing her veil over a face in which the lovely confusion of a sensitive modesty and ardent tenderness still lingered, she suffered the Missionary to place her on the gentle Arabian—and he moving with long and rapid steps by her side, they again renewed their pilgrimage.

Already the bloom and verdure of Cashmire appeared fading into the approaching heights of the sterile Bembhar, and the travellers, silent and thoughtful, ascended those acclivities, which seemed but to reflect the smiling lustre of the scenes they left; no sound, even of nature, disturbed the profound silence of scenes—so still and solemn, that they resembled the primæval world, ere human existence had given animation to its pathless wilds, or human passions had disturbed the calm of its mild tranquillity! No sound was heard, save the jackall's dismal yell, which so often disturbs the impressive and serene beauty of Indian scenery.

But this death-like calm failed to communicate a correspondent influence to the bosom of the solitary wanderers:—again together, in a boundless solitude, they were yet silent, as though they feared a human accent would destroy the impassioned mystery which existed between them; while religion and penitence, and delicacy and self-distrust, enforced the necessity of a reserve, to which both alike submitted with difficulty but with fortitude. Solitude, with the object of a suppressed tenderness, is always too dangerous! and that great passion which seeks a desart, finds the proper region of its own empire. Thus, those helpless and tender friends, in whom love and grace struggled with equal sway, now eagerly looked forward to their restoration to society, which would afford them that protection against themselves, which nature, in her loveliest regions, had hitherto seemed to refuse them.

The travellers at last reached the summit of the *rock of Bembhar*; and, ere they descended the wild and burning plains of Upper Lahore, the Indian turned round to take a last view of her native Eden. The sun was setting in all his majesty of light upon the valley; and villages, and pagodas, and groves, and rivers, were brilliantly tinted with his crimson rays. Luxima cast one look in that direction where lay the district of Sirinaur—another towards Heaven—and then fixed her tearful eyes on the Missionary, with an expression so eloquent and so ardent, that they seemed to say, "Heaven and earth have I resigned for thee!"—The Missionary met and returned her look, but dared not trust his lips to speak; and, in the sympathy and intelligence of that silent glance, the Indian found country, kindred, friends; or ceased for a moment to remember she had lost them all.

Sad, silent, and gloomy, resembling the first pair, when they had reached the boundary of their native paradise, they now descended the southern declivities of Bembhar: the dews of Cashmire no longer embalmed the evening air, and the heated vapours which arose from the plains below, rendered the atmosphere insupportably intense.

As they reached the plains of Upper Lahore, a few dark shrubs and blasted trees alone presented themselves in the hot and sandy soil; and when a stalk of rosemary and lavender, or the scarlet tulip of the desert, tempted the hand of the Missionary, for her to whom flowers were always precious, they mouldered into dust at his touch!

Luxima endeavoured to stifle a sigh, as she beheld nature in this her most awful and destructive aspect—and the Missionary, with a sad smile, sought to cheer her drooping spirit, by pointing out to her the track of the caravan, or the snowy summit of *Mount Alideck*, which arose like a land-mark before them. Having paused for a short time, while the Missionary ascended a rock, to perceive if the caravan was in view—which if it had been, the light of a brilliant moon would have discovered,—they proceeded during the night, in sadness and in gloom, while the intense thirst produced by the ardour of the air had already exhausted the juicy fruits with which the Missionary had supplied himself for Luxima's refreshment; at last the faint glimmering of the stars was lost in the brighter lustre of the morning-planet; the resplendent herald of day, riding in serene lustre through the heavens, ushered in the vigorous sun, whose potent rays rapidly pervaded the whole horizon.—The fugitives found themselves near a large and solitary edifice; it was a *Choultry*, built for the shelter of travellers, and, as an inscription indicated, "built by *Luxima*, the *Prophetess and Bramachira of Cashmire*!"—At the sight of this object, the Indian turned pale—all the glory and happiness of her past life rushed on the recollection of the excommunicated Chancalas; and her guide, feeling in all their force the sacrifices which she had made for him, silently and tenderly chased away her tears, with her veil. As it was impossible to proceed during the meridional ardours of the day, the wearied and exhausted Indian sought shelter and repose beneath that roof which her own charity had raised; and a cocoa-tree, planted on the edge of a tank which she had excavated, afforded to her that refreshment, which she had benevolently provided for others. Here, it was evident, the caravan had lately halted; for the remains of some provisions, usually left by Indian travellers for those who may succeed them, were visible, and the track of wheels, of horses, and of camels' feet, was every where apparent. Revived and invigorated by an hour's undisturbed repose, they again re-commenced their route; still pursuing the track of the caravan, while, in forms rendered indistinct by distance, they still fancied they beheld the object of their pursuit. Scenes more varied than those through which they had already journeyed, now presented themselves to their view. Sometimes they passed through a ruined village, which the flame of war had desolated; sometimes beneath the remains of a Mogul fortress, whose mouldering arches presented the most picturesque specimens of eastern military architecture; while from the marshy fosse, which surrounded the majestic ruins, arose a bright blue flame, and moving with velocity amidst its mouldering bastions, floating like waves, or falling like sparks of fire, became suddenly extinct—Luxima gazed upon this spectacle with fear and amazement, and, governed by the superstition of her early education, saw, in a natural phenomenon, the effects of a supernatural agency; trembling, she clung to her pastor and her guide, and said, "It is the spirit of one who fell in the battle, or who died in the defence of these ruins, and who, for some crime unredeemed, is thus destined to wander till the time of expiation is accomplished, and he return into some form on earth."

The Missionary sought to release her mind from the bondage of imaginary terrors, and at once to amuse her fancy, to enlighten her ideas, and to elevate her soul; he explained to her, with ingenious simplicity, the various and wonderful modes by which the Divine Spirit disposes of the different powers of nature, still teaching her to feel "God in all, and all in God."

Luxima gazed on him with wonder while he spoke, and hung in silent admiration on words she deemed inspired; yet when, as it sometimes occurred, she beheld the rude altars raised, even in the most unfrequented places to *Boom-Daivee*, the goddess of the earth[3]; or to the Daivadergoel, the tutelar guardians of wilds and forests, her senses acknowledged these images of her antient superstition, in spite of her reason, and she involuntarily bowed before the objects of her habitual devotion. Then the Missionary reproved her severely for the perpetual vacillation of her undecided faith; but, disarming his severity by looks and words of tenderness, she would

[3] See Kindersley's History of the Hindu Mythology.

fondly reply—"Oh! my Father! it is not all devotion which bows my head and bends my knee before these well remembered shrines of my antient faith! Alas! it is not all a pious impulse, but a natural sympathy: for the genii to whom these altars are raised, were once, as I was, happy and glorified; but they incurred the wrath of *Shiven*,[4] by abandoning his laws; and, banished from their native heaven, were doomed to wander in solitary wastes to expiate their error:—but here, that sympathy ceases; for they found not, like me, a compensation for the paradise they forfeited; *they* found not on earth, something which partook of heaven, and they knew not that perfect communion, which images to the soul, in its transient probation through time, the bliss which awaits it in eternity."

It was by words like these, timidly and tenderly pronounced, that the feelings of the spiritual guide were put to the most severe test; it was words like these, which chilled his which increased the hidden sentiment, manner, while they warmed his heart; and restrained the external emotion, and which cherished and fed his passion, while they awakened his self-distrust: but Luxima, at once his peril and his salvation, counteracted by her innocence the effects of her tenderness, and alternately awakened, excited or subdued, by that feminine display of feeling and sentiment, which blended purity with ardour, and elevation of soul with tenderness of heart. More sensitive than reflecting, she was guided rather by an instinctive delicacy, than a prudent reserve; in *her*, sentiment supplied the place of reason, and she was the most virtuous, because she was the most affectionate of women.

The evening again arose upon their wanderings, and they paused ere they proceeded to encounter the pathless way through the gloom of night; they paused near the edge of a spring, which afforded a delicious refreshment; and, under the shadow of a lofty tamarind-tree, which, blooming in solitary beauty, supplied at once both fruit and shade, and seemed dropt in the midst of a lonesome waste, as a beacon to hope, as an assurance of the providential care of *him*, who reared its head in the desert for the relief of his creatures. Here the Missionary left Luxima to take repose; and, having fastened the *Arabian* to a neighbouring rock, embossed with patches of vegetation, he

[4] "C'est dans le *Shasta* que l'on trouve 'histoire de la Chute des Anges."—*Essai sur les Mœurs des Nations. P. 2, T. 2.*

proceeded across some stoney acclivities which were covered by the caprice of nature with massy clumps of the *bamboo tree*. When he had reached the opposite side, he looked back to catch, as he was wont, a glimpse of Luxima; but, for the first time since the commencement of their pilgrimage, she was hidden from his view by the intervening foliage of the plantation, trembling at the fancied dangers which might assail her in his absence: he proceeded with a rapid step towards an eminence, in the hope of ascertaining, from its summit, the path of the caravan, or of discovering some human habitation, though but the hut of a *pariah*, whose owner might guide their now uncertain steps. Turning his eyes towards the still glowing West, he perceived a forest whose immense trees marked their waving outline on saffron clouds, which hung radiantly upon their gloom, tinging their dark branches with the yellow lustre of declining light; he perceived also, that this awful and magnificent forest was skirted by an illimitable jungle, through whose long-entangled grass a broad path-way seemed to have been recently formed, and, vision growing strong by exercise, the first confusion of objects which had distracted his gaze, gradually subsiding into distinct images, he perceived the blue smoke curling from a distant hut, which he knew, from its desolate situation, to be the miserable residence of some *Indian outcast*; he soon more distinctly observed some great body in motion: at first it appeared compact and massive; by degrees broken and irregular; and at last the form and usual pace of a troop of camels were obvious to his far-stretched sight, by a deep red light which suddenly illumined the whole firmament, and, throwing its extended beams into the distant fore-ground, fell, with bright tints, upon every object, and confirmed the Missionary in hopes, he almost trembled to encourage, that the caravan at that moment moved before his eyes! But the joy was yet imperfect; unshared by *her*, who was now identified with all his hopes and all his fears; and descending the hill with the rapidity of lightning, he suddenly perceived his steps impeded by a phenomenon which at first seemed some sudden vision of the fancy, to which the senses unresistingly submitted; for a brilliant circle of fire gradually extending, forbid his advance, and had illuminated, by its kindling light, the surrounding atmosphere! Recovering from the first emotion of horror and consternation, his knowledge of the natural history of the country soon informed him of the cause of the apparent miracle[5], without reconciling him to its effects; he

[5] This singular spectacle frequently presents itself to the eye of the traveller in the

perceived that the *bamboos*, violently agitated by a strong and sultry wind, which suddenly arose from the South, and crept among their branches, had produced a violent friction in their dry stalks, which emitted sparks of fire, and which, when communicated to their leaves, produced on their summits one extended blaze, which was now gradually descending to their trunks. Though this extraordinary spectacle fulfilled, rather than violated, a law of nature, the Missionary's heart, struck by the obstacle it opposed to his wishes and his views, and the terrors it held out to his imagination, felt as if, by some interposition of Divine wrath, he had been separated, for ever, from her who had thus armed Heaven against him. Given up to a distraction which knew no bounds from reason or religion, he accused the Eternal Judge, who, in making the object of his error the cause of his retribution, had not proportioned his punishment to his crime, and who had implicated in the vengeance which bowed *him* to the earth, a creature free and innocent of voluntary error.—Yet, considering less his own sufferings, than the probable and impending destruction of Luxima, thus exposed, alone, in solitary deserts, to want! to the inclemency of treacherous elements! to the fury of savage beasts! perhaps to men, scarce less savage! who might refuse her that protection, their very presence rendered necessary—his mind and feelings were roused, even to frenzy, by the frightful images conjured up by a heart distracted for the safety of its sole object; and the instinct of self-preservation, that strong and almost indestructible instinct, submitted to the paramount influence of a *sentiment*; but that sentiment before which nature stood checked, blended the united passions of *love* and *pity*, the best and dearest which fill the human breast—and, resolved to risk his life for the salvation of hers, dearer to him still than life,—he threw around him a rapid glance, in the faint hope of discerning some object which might assist him in the perilous enterprise he meditated, and enable him to encounter the rage of those flames which opposed his return to the goal of his solicitude and anxiety. It was then he perceived that the surrounding rocks were covered with the entangled web of the *mountain flax*, the inconsumable *amianthus* of India.[6]

---

hilly parts of the Carnatic, as well as in Upper India, particularly about the *Ghauts*, which are covered with the bamboo tree.

[6] One of the varieties of the *asbestos*, which when long exposed to air, dissolves into a downy matter, unassailable by common fire.

At this sight, the providential care of the Divinity, who every where presents an *antidote* to that evil which may eventually become the bane of human preservation, smote his heart—and, raising his soul and eyes in thankfulness to Heaven, he wrapped round his uncovered head, the fibres of this singular and indestructible fossile, and, folding his robe closely round his body, he plunged daringly forward, throwing aside the branches of the burning trees, which flamed above his head, with the iron point of his crosier, as he flew over the arid path, and looking as he moved like the mighty *spirit* of that *element* to which the popular superstition of the region he inhabited would have offered its homage.[7] The fire had nearly exhausted itself in the direction in which he moved, and soon left nothing but its smoking embers to impede his course. Scorched, spent, and almost deprived of respiration, he reached the opposite side of the plantation, and, with the recovery of breath and strength, he flew towards the spot where he had left his charge, whom every new peril, by adding anxiety to love, bound more closely to his heart. He found her wrapt in profound slumber; the moon-light, checquered by the branches of the tree through which it fell, played on her face and bosom; but her figure was in deep shade, from its position; and a disciple of her own faith would have worshipped her, had he passed, and said, " 'Tis the messenger of Heaven,[8] who bears to earth the mandate of *Vishnoo*;" for it is thus the Indian *Iris* is sometimes mystically represented—nothing visible of its beauty, but the countenance of a youthful seraph. Close to the brow of the innocent slumberer lay, in many a mazy fold, a serpent of immense size: his head, crested and high, rose erect; his scales of verdant gold glittered to the moon-light, and his eyes bright and fierce were fixed on the victim, whose first motion might prove the signal of her death. These two objects, so singular in their association, were alone conspicuous in the scene, which was elsewhere hid in the massive shadows of the projecting branches. At the sight of this image, so beautiful and so terrific, so awfully fine, so grandly dreadful, where loveliness and death, and peace and destruction, were so closely blended, the distracted and solitary spectator stood aghast!—A chill of horror running through his veins, his joints relaxed; his limbs, transfixed and faint, cold and powerless, fearing lest his very respiration might accelerate the dreadful fate which thus hung

[7] *Augne-Baugauvin*, the God of Fire, and one of the eight keepers of the world.

[8] Saindovoer.

over the sole object and tie of his existence,—breathless, motionless,—he wore the perfect semblance of that horrible suspense, which fills the awful interval between impending death, and lingering life! Twice he raised his crosier to hurl it at the serpent's head; and twice his arm fell nerveless back, while his shuddering heart doubted the certain aim of his trembling hand,—and whether, in attempting to strike at the vigilant reptile, he might not reach the bosom of his destined victim, and urge him to her immediate destruction!—But, feelings so acute were not long to be endured: cold drops fell from his brow, his inflamed eye had gazed itself into dimness, increasing agony became madness,—and, unable to resist the frenzy of his thronging emotions, he raised the pastoral spear, and had nearly hurled it at the destroyer, when his arm was checked by a sound which seemed to come from Heaven, breathing hope and life upon his soul; for it operated with an immediate and magic influence on the organs of the reptile, who suddenly drooped his crested head, and, extending wide his circling folds, wound his mazy course, in many an indented wave, towards that point, where some seeming impulse of the "vocal aid" lured his nature from its prey.

Luxima slowly awakening from her sweet repose, to sounds too well remembered, for it was the vesper hymn of the Indian huntsmen, raised her head upon her arm, and threw wildly round her the look of one wrapt in visionary trance—now resting her eye upon the Missionary, who stood before her motionless, suspended between joy and horror, between fear and transport—now upon the flaming circles which hung upon the burning *bamboos*—and now on the receding serpent, whose tortuous train, veering as he moved, still glistened brightly on the earth, till slowly following the fainting sounds, his voluble and lengthening folds were lost in the deep shade of a sombre thicket;—then the Indian raised her hands and eyes to heaven in thankfulness to that Power who had mercifully saved her from a dreadful death. The music ceased; nature had reached the crisis of emotion in the breast of the Missionary: without power to articulate or to move, he bent one knee to the earth; he raised his folded hands to Heaven; but his eyes were turned on the object of its protection: he sighed out her name, and Luxima was in a moment at his side.

Chapter XIV.

THE left arm of the Missionary had suffered from the flames; Luxima was the first to perceive it: she applied to it the only remedy which nature afforded them in a spot so desolate; and the ingenuity of love, and of necessity, supplied the place of skill. She gathered from the neighbouring spring, the oily *naptha*, whose volatile and subtil fluid so frequently floats on the surface of Indian wells, and, steeping in it the fragment of her veil, she bound it round the arm of her patient. Thus engaged, the thoughts of the wanderers, by a natural association, mutually reverted to their first interview in the grotto of Congelations; when the rigid distinctions of prejudice first gave way to an impulse of humanity, and the Priestess of Brahma, no less in fear than pity, bound up the wound of him whom she then deemed it a sacrilege to approach! The sympathy of the recollection was visible in the disorder of their looks, which were studiously averted from each other; and the Neophyte, endeavouring to turn the thoughts of her spiritual guide from a subject she trembled to revert to, spoke of the danger which he had recently incurred for her sake, and spoke of it with all the fervour which characterized her eloquence.

The Missionary replied with the circumspect reserve of one who feared to trust his feelings: he said, "That which I have done *for thee*, I would have done for another, for it is the spirit of the religion I profess, to sacrifice the selfish instinct of our nature to the preservation of a fellow-creature whose danger claims our interference, or whose happiness needs our protection."

"Oh! Father," she returned in emotion, "refer not to thy faith alone, a sentiment inherent in thyself; let us be more just *to him* who made us, and believe, that there is in nature, a feeling of benevolence which betrays the original intention of the Deity, to promote the happiness of his creatures. If thou art prone to pity the wretched, and aid the weak, it is because thou wast thyself created of those particles which, at an infinite distance, constitute the Divine essence."

The Missionary interrupted her by a look of reprehension; he knew such was the doctrine, and such the phrase of the Brahmins, with respect to those of their holy men who led a religious and sinless life: but he felt, at the moment, how little claim he had to make any application of it to himself.

"Thy religion, at least," continued Luxima, with softness and timidity, "forbids not the expression of *gratitude*. It is said in the Shaster, that the first thought of Brahma, when created by the great Spirit, was a sentiment of gratitude; he offered up thanks to the Author of his existence, for the gift of life, and a reasonable soul: is then the Christian doctrine less amiable than that I have abandoned? and, if through thee, my life has been preserved, and my soul enlightened, must I stifle in my heart, the gratitude thou hast awakened there?"

"Luxima" exclaimed the Missionary, with vehemence, "*all* sentiments merely of the heart are dangerous, and to be distrusted; whatever soothes the passions, tends to cherish them,—whatever affords pleasure, endangers virtue,—and even the love we bear to Heaven, we should try, were it possible, to separate from the happiness which that love confers Oh! Luxima, it is a dangerous habit,—the habit of enjoying any earthly good, and until now—" he broke off suddenly, and sighed, then added, "Thou talkest much of gratitude, Luxima; but wherefore? It was for Heaven I sought thee—it is for Heaven I saved thee! It was not for *thy* sake, nor for mine, that I lured thee from the land of the unbelieving, or that I would risk a thousand lives to save thine,—it is for *his* sake, whose servant I am. But, if *thou* talkest of gratitude, to whom is it due? *Art thou not here?* in dreary deserts, encompassed round by danger and by death: to follow me, thou art here,—thou, the native of an earthly paradise,—the idol of a nation's homage. Oh! I should have left thy pure soul, all innocent as it was of voluntary error, to return to its Creator, untried by the dangers, unassailed by the tempting evils of passion and of life, virtuous in thy illusions, pure from the errors and misfortunes of humanity, an inmate fit for the Heaven which awaited thee."

"Be that Heaven my witness," returned Luxima, with devotion and solemnity, "that I would not for the happiness I have abandoned, and the glory I have lost, resign that desert, whose perilous solitudes I share with thee. Oh! my father, and my friend, thou alone hast taught me to know, that the paradise of woman is the creation of her heart; that it is not the light or air of Heaven, though beaming brightness, and breathing fragrance, nor all that is loveliest in nature's scenes, which form the *sphere* of *her* existence and enjoyment!—it is alone the presence of *him she loves*: it is that mysterious sentiment of the heart, which diffuses a finer sense of life through the whole being; and which resembles, in its singleness and simplicity, the *primordial idea*, which, in the religion of my fathers, is supposed to have preceded *time* and *worlds*, and from which all created good has emanated."

The Missionary arose, in disorder; he turned, for a moment, his eyes on Luxima: the glow which mantled to her brow, the bashful confusion of her look, the modesty with which she drew her veil over her downcast eyes, spoke the involuntary error of one, whose ardent feelings had for a moment over-ruled the circumspect reserve of a rigid virtue. He sighed profoundly, and withdrew his glance. Luxima now also arose; and they were both proceeding on in silence, when a rustling in the thicket was distinctly heard, and the next moment a large but meagre dog sprang forward, followed by an Indian, on whose dark and melancholy countenance the light of the moon fell brightly; a scanty garment, woven of the fibres of trees, partially concealed his slender and worn form; an Indian pipe was suspended from his girdle; and he leaned, as he paused, to gaze on the wanderers, upon a huntsman's *spear*. But, scarcely had he fixed his haggard eyes on the brow of Luxima, which still bore the consecrated *mark of the tellertum*,[9] than he fell prostrate on the earth, in token of reverential homage. Luxima shrieked, and hiding her head in the bosom of the Missionary, exclaimed "Let us fly, or we are lost! it is a *pariah*!"

---

[9] The *tellertum* is a mark which is at once an ornament and an indication of cast and religious profession.

The *unfortunate*, rising from the earth, and withdrawing a few paces, said, in a timid and respectful accent:—"I am indeed of that wretched cast, who live under the curse of Heaven—an outcast! an alien! I claim no country, I *own no kindred*; but still I am human, and can pity in others the suffering I myself endure: I ask not the daughter of Heaven, who sprang from the head of Brahma, to repose beneath the roof of a pariah; but I will conduct her to a spot less perilous than this, and I will lay at her feet the pulp of the young cocoa-nut, which grows by the side of my hut; and when the morning star dawns above yonder forest, I will guide her steps to a path of safety, and teach her how to shun the abode of the wild beast, and to avoid the nest of the serpent."

To these humane offers, Luxima replied only by tears: an *outcast* herself, the unconquerable prejudice and religious pride of the cast she had forfeited, still operated with unabated influence on her mind, and she shuddered when she beheld the Missionary stretch out his hands and press in their grateful clasp those of the unfortunate and benevolent *pariah*: he had been the saviour of the life of her he loved; for it was the music of his sylvan reed, which had seduced the serpent from his prey, and the point of his spear was still red with the blood of the reptile he had destroyed.[10]

But for the first time, neither the example nor the persuasions of the Missionary had any effect upon the mind of his neophyte. Suddenly awakened to all the tyranny of habitual prejudice and superstitious fear, she rejected the repose and safety to be found beneath the shadow of a pariah's *hut*, she rejected the fruit planted by a pariah's hand; and the pride of a Brahmin's daughter, and the bigotry of a Brahmin priestess, still governed the conduct of the excommunicated *chancalas*, still over-ruled the reason of the Christian neophyte: accepting, therefore, only the advice of the unhappy pariah, who directed them to a woody path, by which they might soonest gain the caravan road, and who taught them how to avoid whatever was most dangerous in these unfrequented wilds, they again re-commenced their wanderings. The Missionary, with difficulty guiding the Arabian

[10] According to the *Abbé* Guy on, there is in India a species of serpent, which even in the pursuit of its prey is to be lulled into a profound slumber by the sounds of *musical instruments*. The Indian serpent-hunters frequently make use of this artifice, that they may destroy them with greater facility.

through the intricacies of the forest-path, remained silent and thoughtful; while Luxima, fearing that she had displeased him by an unconquerable obstinacy, which had its foundation in the earliest habits and feelings of her life, sought to cheer his mind and amuse his attention by the repetition of some of those mythological romances, which had formed a part of her professional acquirements. But the Missionary, alive to dangers which in his society *she* felt not, and borne down by the recent disappointment of his flattering hopes, of which *she* was ignorant, gave not to her brilliant and eloquent details, the wonted look of half-repressed transport, the wonted reserved smile of tenderness and admiration; his whole thoughts rested in a faint expectation of overtaking the caravan, which moved slowly, and which had taken a more circuitous road than that to which the pariah had directed him.

In the unfrequented wilds through which they now passed, no trace of human life appeared, save that once, and at an immense distance, they beheld the arms of some Indian troops glittering brightly to the moon-beams; but the welcome spectacle passed away like a midnight phantom; and, that again they observed a circle of glimmering fires, before which the remote shadows of an elephant's form seemed to pass. Luxima, acquainted with the customs of her country, believed this spectacle to belong to a hunting match of elephants; a diversion in India truly royal. At last, having recovered the traces of the caravan, which were deeply impressed on the soil, they found themselves on a wild and marshy waste, skirted by the impenetrable forest, from whose gloom they now emerged;—the earth trembled beneath their sinking feet, and particles of light arising from putrescent substances, rose like meteors before them; while frequently the high jungle grass, almost surmounting the lofty figure of the Missionary, stubbornly resisted the efforts which he made with his extended arms to clear a passage for the animal on which Luxima was mounted;—the moon, suddenly absorbed in clouds, left them with "*danger and with darkness compassed round*;"—while the low and sullen murmurs of the elements foretold a rising storm. Exhausted by heat and by fatigue, no longer able to perceive the track of the caravan, the unfortunate wanderers sought only to avoid the dreadful inclemency of the moment: sounds of horror mingled in the wild expanse; the hiss of serpents, and the yell of ferocious animals which instinctively sought shelter amidst the profound depths of the forest, (whose mighty trees, bending their summits to the sweeping blast, rolled like billows in deep and dying murmurs) all around bowed as in awful reverence to the omnipotent voice of nature, thus pouring her accents of terror in the deep roll of endless thunder; the crash of shattered rocks, the groans of torn-up trees, and all those images of terror which mark the *land-tempests* in those mighty regions, where even destruction wears an aspect of magnificence and sublimity, all struck upon the soul of the fainting Indian, and left there an impression never to be effaced. It was then that the religion which she had abandoned, less from *conviction* than from *love*, and the superstitious errors which were still latent in her mind, resumed at this moment (to her, of dreadful retribution) all their former influence; and she felt the wrath of Heaven in every flash of lightning which darted round her head: for the mind long devoted to an illusion interwoven with all its ideas, however it may abandon its influence in the repose of safety, or the blessings of enjoyment, still clings to it, as to a resource, in suffering and in danger; and, contrite for the transient apostacy, adds the energy of repentance to the zeal of returning faith.

The Missionary, who beheld remorse in the bosom of his proselyte strengthening under the dangers which had awakened it, in vain endeavoured to soothe and to support her; she shrank from his arms, and, prostrate on the earth, invoked those deities whom she still believed to have been the tutelar guardians of the days of her innocence and her felicity; while he, still feeling only through her, stood near to shield and to protect her: awed, but not subdued, he presented a fine image of the majesty of man;—his brow fearlessly raised to meet the lightning's flash, a blasted tree in ruins at his feet, and while all lay desolate and in destruction round him, looking like one whose spirit, unsubdued by the mighty wreck of matter, defied that threatened annihilation, which could not reach the immortality it was created to inherit!

The storm ceased in a tremendous crash of the elements, with all the abrupt grandeur with which it had arisen; and a breathless calm, scarcely less awful, succeeded to its violence; the clouds dispersed from the face of the Heavens, and the moon, full and cloudless, rose in the firmament:

every thing urged the departure of the wanderers, for danger, in various forms, surrounded them.—Luxima, alive to every existing impression, was cheered even by the solemn calm, but nearly exhausted and overcome by suffering and fatigue, the Missionary was obliged to support her on the horse; and though she tried to smile, yet her silent tears, and uncomplaining sufferings, relaxed the firmness of his mind; he felt, that, were even her conversion perfected, which he hourly discovered it was far from being, she would have purchased the sacred truths of Christianity at the dearest price, and that Heaven alone could compensate the unhappy and apostate Indian, who thus sought it at the expence of every earthly good and human happiness.

At length the trees of the forest, on whose remotest skirts they wandered, gradually disappeared; and, still following the track of the caravan, which in the course of the night they had again recovered as well as the moon's declining light would permit, they crossed a hill, where it seemed by its impressions on the soil recently to have passed: they then descended into a boundless plain, dismal, wild, and waste. Ere the sun had risen in all its fiercest glories above the horizon, they found themselves surrounded by a desert: the guiding track indeed still remained; but, in the illimitable waste, far as the eye could stretch its view, no object which could cheer their hearts, or dispel their fears, presented itself:—sky and earth alone appeared, alike awful, and alike unvaried; the heavens, shrouded with a deep red gloom, spread a boundless canopy to the view, like the concave roof of some earth-embosomed mine, whose golden veins shine duskily in gloomy splendour; and the sandy and burning soil, unvaried by a single tree or shrub, reflected back the scorching ardour of the skies, and mingled its brilliant surface with the distant horizon; both alike were terrific to the fancy, and boundless to the eye; both alike struck horror on the mind, and chased hope from the heart; alike denying all resource, withholding all relief; while the disconsolate wanderers, as they trod the burning waste, now turned their looks on the bleak perspective, now tenderly and despairingly on each other. Convinced that to return or to advance threatened alike destruction, thus they continued to wander in the lonesome and desolate wild, enduring the intense heat of the ardent day, the noxious blast of the chilly night, with no shelter from the horrors of the clime but what a clump of naked rocks at intervals afforded them; and when this rude asylum presented itself, the Missionary spread his robe on the earth for Luxima—endeavouring to soothe her to repose, only leaving her side to seek some spring, always vainly sought, or to look for those hardy shrubs which even the desert sometimes produces, and which frequently treasure in their flowers the lingering dews of moister seasons; if he found them, it was mouldering amidst the dry red sand of the soil. At last the delicate animal, which had hitherto afforded them so much relief and aid, sunk beneath the intemperature of the clime, and expired at their feet. Luxima was now borne hopelessly along by the associate and the cause of her sufferings; and they proceeded slowly and despairingly, their parched and burning lips, their wearied and exhausted frames, scarcely permitting them to speak without effort, or to move without pain. But it was for Luxima only the Missionary suffered—he saw her whom he had found in the possession of every enjoyment, now almost expiring beneath his eyes; her lips of roses, scorched by the noxious blasts, and gust after gust of burning vapour, drying up the vital springs of life; while she, confounding in her mind her afflictions, and what she believed to be their cause, offered up faint invocations to appease those powers, whom love had induced her thus to provoke and to abandon.

It was in moments such as these, that the unfortunate Hilarion beheld that hope frustrated, which had hitherto solaced him in all the sufferings he had caused, and those he sustained; it was then that he felt it was the heart of the woman he had seduced, and not the mind of the heathen he had converted. At last, wholly overcome by the intense heat and immoderate fatigue, by insupportable thirst and a long privation of sustenance and sleep, Luxima was unable to proceed. The Missionary bore her in his feeble clasp to the base of a rock, which afforded them some shelter from the rays of the sun. He would have spoken to her of the Heaven to which her soul seemed already taking its flight; he would have assured her that his spirit would soon mingle with hers, and that an eternal union awaited them: but, in a moment, when love was strengthened by mutual suffering, and despair gave force to passion, and when each at once only lived and died for the other, words were poor vehicles to feelings so acute; and sighs, long and deep drawn, were the only sounds which emotions so profound, so tender, and so agonizing, would admit of: all was the silence of love unspeakable, and the awful stillness of dissolution. But when over the beautiful countenance which lay on his bosom, the Missionary beheld the sudden convulsion of pain throw its dread distortion,—madness seized the brain of the frantic lover, and he threw round a look wild and inquiring, but looked in vain; all was still, hopeless, and desolate. At last, something like a vapour appeared moving at a distance. He sprung forward, and, ascending the point of a rock, discovered at a distance a form which resembled that of a camel: faint as was the hope now awakened, it spread new life through his whole being; he snatched the dying Indian to his bosom; strength and velocity seemed a supernatural gift communicated to his frame; he flew over the burning sand, he approached the object of his wishes; hope with every step realizes the blessed vision; human forms grew distinct on his eye, human sounds vibrate on his ear—"She lives, she is saved!" he exclaims with a frantic shriek, and falls lifeless beneath his precious burthen in the midst of the multitude which forms the rear of the caravan. The caravan had stopped in this place near a spring, accidentally discovered, and the motley crowd which composed it, were all verging towards one point, eagerly contending for a draught of muddy water; but the sudden and extraordinary appearance of the now almost lifeless strangers, excited an emotion in all who beheld them. The few Hindus who belonged to the caravan shrank in horror from the unfortunate *Chancalas*, thus so closely associated with a *frangui*, or impure; but those in whom religious bigotry had no deadened the feelings of nature, beheld them with equal pity and admiration. Every assistance which humanity could devise was administered; and cordials, diluted with water, moistened lips parched with a long consuming thirst, and recalled to frames nearly exhausted, the fading powers of life. The Missionary, more overcome by his anxiety for Luxima, and the sudden transition of his feelings from despair to hope, than even by weakness, or personal suffering, was the first to recover consciousness and strength, and love instinctively claimed the first thought of reviving existence. In the transport of the moment he forgot the crowd that was its witness; he flew to Luxima, and shed tears of love and joy on the hands extended to him. He beheld the vital hues revisiting that cheek which he had lately pressed in hopeless agony, and saw the light of life beaming in those eyes whose lustre he had so lately seen darkened by the shades of death. Again, too, the voice of Luxima addresses him by the endearing epithet of "Father:" and though the venerated title found no sanction in their looks or years, yet many who beheld the scene of their re-union were touched by its affecting tenderness; and a general interest was excited for persons so noble, and so distinguished in their appearance, so interesting by their sufferings and misfortunes, which were registered in their looks, and attested by the singularity of their situations.

Chapter XV.

LUXIMA, restored to life, was still feeble and exhausted: but though faded, she was still lovely; and, being immediately recognized as a *Hindu*, that peculiar circumstance awakened curiosity and surmise. Those of her own nation and religion still shrank from her in horror, and declared her to be a *Chancalas*, or outcast; the Moslems who beheld her, sought not to conceal their rude admiration, and recognized her at once for a *Cashmirian* by her complexion and her beauty; but the persons who seemed to observe her with most scrutiny, were *two Europeans*, whose features were concealed by hoods, worn apparently to shade off the ardour of the sun. Luxima was permitted to share the *mohaffah* or litter of a female seik who was going with her husband, a dealer in gems, to Tatta. The Missionary was suffered to ascend the back of a camel, whose proprietor had expired the day before in the desert. Having declared himself a Portuguese of distinction, a Christian missionary, and shewed the briefs which testified his rank, he found no difficulty in procuring such necessaries as were requisite for the rest of their journey, until his arrival at Tatta should enable him to defray the debt of obligation which he of necessity incurred.

But though he had declared the nature of the relation in which he stood to his Neophyte to those immediately about him, yet he fancied, that the fact was, received by some with suspicion, and by others with incredulity. He was evidently considered the seducer of the fugitive Indian; and neither his innocence nor his dignity could save him from a profound mortification, new and insupportable to his proud and lofty nature: yet, trembling to observe the admiration which Luxima inspired, he still hovered near her in ceaseless disquietude and anxiety. The caravan was composed of five hundred persons of various nations and religions;—Mogul pilgrims, going from India to visit the tomb of their prophet at Mecca; merchants from Thibet and China, carrying the produce of their native climes, the Western coasts of Hindostan; Seiks, the Swiss of the East, going to join the forces of rebelling Rajahs; and faquirs and dervises, who rendered religion profitable by carrying for sale in their girdles, spices, gold-dust, and musk. Luxima, obviously abhorred by those of her own religion, closely observed by some, and suspected by all, felt her situation equally through her sex and her prejudices, and shrunk from the notice she unavoidably attracted in shame and in confusion: it was now that her forfeiture of cast for the first time appeared to the Missionary in all its horrors, and he no longer wondered that so long as the prejudice existed, with which it is connected, it should hold so tyrannic an influence over the Indian mind. His tenderness increasing with his pity, and his jealousy of those who attempted to approach, or to address her, giving a new force and character to his passion, he seldom left the side of her *litter*: yet he endeavoured to moderate the warmth of feelings it was now more than ever necessary to conceal. That passion, dangerous in every situation, was now no longer solitary as the wilds in which it sprang, but connected with society, and exposed to its observation; and the reserve with which he sought to temper its ardour, restored to it all that mysterious delicacy, which constitutes, perhaps, its first, and perhaps its best charm.

The caravan proceeded on its route, and, having passed the Desert, crossed the *Setlege*, and entered the *Moultan*, it halted at one of its usual stations, and the tents of the travellers were pitched on the shores of the Indus: the perils of the past were no longer remembered, and the safety of the present was ardently enjoyed; while the views and interests of the motley multitude, no longer subdued by personal danger, or impeded by personal suffering, again operated with their original force and activity. The merchants bartered with the traders, who came from the surrounding towns for the purpose; and the professors of the various religions and sects preached their respective doctrines to those whom they wished to convert, or to those who already believed, all but the Christian Missionary! Occupied by feelings of a doubtful and conflicting nature, sometimes hovering round the tent which Luxima shared with the family of the Seik, sometimes buried in profound thought, and wandering amidst the depths of a neighbouring forest, where he sought to avoid the idle bustle of those among whom he was adventitiously thrown; anxious, unquiet, and distrustful even of himself, he was now lost to that evangelic peace of mind, to that sober tranquillity of feeling, so indispensable to the exercise of his mission. Though buried in a reserve which awed, while it distanced, there was a majesty in his air, and a dignified softness in his manner, which daily increased that popular interest in his favour, which his first appearance had awakened: to this he was not insensible; for, still ambitious of distinction as saint or as man, he beheld his influence with a triumph natural to one, who, emulous of unrivalled superiority, feels that he owes it not to extraneous circumstance, but to that proud and indefeasible right of supreme eminence, with which nature has endowed him. But he could not but particularly observe, that he was an object of singular attention to the two European travellers, who, wrapped in mystery, seemed to shun all intercourse, and avoid all observation; and, though they crossed him in his solitary walks, pursued him to the entrance of Luxima's tent, and hung upon his every word and action, yet so subtilely had they eluded his notice, that he had not yet obtained an opportunity of either distinctly seeing their features, or of addressing them; all he could learn was, that they had joined the caravan from *Lahore*, with two other persons of the same dress and description as themselves, who had proceeded with the advanced troop of the caravan, and that they were known to be Europeans and Christians. It was not till the caravan had entered the province of *Sindy*, that one of them, who rode near the camel of the Missionary, seemed inclined to address him; after some observations he said, "It is understood that you are a Christian Missionary! but, while in this mighty multitude the professor of each false religion appears anxious to advance his doctrine, and to promulgate his creed, how is it that the *apostle of Christianity* is alone silent and indifferent on the subject of that pure faith, to the promulgation of which he has devoted himself?"—

The Missionary threw a haughty look over the figure of the person who thus interrogated him; but, with a sudden recollection, he endeavoured to recall the humility of his religious character, and replied: "The question is natural—and the silence to which you allude is not the effect of weakened zeal, nor the result of abated enthusiasm, in the sacred cause to which I have devoted myself—it is a silence which arises from a consciousness that though I spoke with the tongues of angels, it *would be here but as the sound of tinkling brass*; for *truth*, which always prevails over unbiassed ignorance, has ever failed in its effect upon bigoted error—and the dogma most difficult to vanquish, is that which is guarded by self-interest."

"You allude to the obstinate paganism of the Brahmins?"

"I allude to the power of the most powerful of all human superstitions; a superstition which equally presides over the heavenly hope, and directs the temporal concern; and which so intimately blends itself with all the relations of human life, as equally to dictate a doctrinal tenet, or a sumptuary law, to regulate alike the salvation of the soul, and fix the habits of existence."

"It is the peculiar character of the zeal of Christianity to rise in proportion to the obstacles it encounters!"

"The zeal of Christianity should never forsake the mild spirit of its fundamental principles; in the excess of its warmest enthusiasm, it should be tempered by charity, guided by reason, and regulated by possibility; forsaken by these, it ceases to be the zeal of religion, and becomes the spirit of fanaticism, tending only to sever man from man, and to multiply the artificial sources of aversion by which human society is divided, and human happiness destroyed!"

"This temperance in doctrine, argues a freedom in opinion, and a languor in zeal, which rather belongs to the character of the heathen philosophy, than to the enthusiasm of Christian faith; had its disciples been always thus moderate, thus languid, thus philosophically tolerant, never would the cross have been raised upon the remotest shores of the Eastern and Western oceans!"

"Too often has it been raised under the influence of a sentiment diametrically opposite to the spirit of the doctrine of him who *suffered on it*, and who came not to *destroy*, but to *save* mankind. Too often has it been raised by those whose minds were guided by an evil and interested policy, fatal to the effects which it sought to accomplish, and who lifted to Heaven, hands stained with the blood of those, to whom they had been sent to preach the religion of peace, of love, and of salvation; for even the zeal of religion, when animated by human passions, may become fatal in its excess, and that daring fanaticism, which gives force and activity to the courage of the man, may render merciless and atrocious, the zeal of the bigot."

"You disapprove then of that energy of conversion which either by art or force secures or redeems the soul from the sin of idolatry?"

"*Force* and *art* may indeed effect profession, but cannot induce the conviction of faith; for the individual perception of truth is not to be effected by the belief of others, and an act of faith must be either an act of private judgment, or of free will, which no human artifice, no human authority can alter or controul."

"You disapprove then of the zealous exertions of the Jesuits in the cause of Christianity, and despair of their success?"

"I disapprove not of the zeal, but of the mediums by which it manifests itself: I believe that the coercion and the artifice to which they resort, frequently impel the Hindus to a resistance, which they perhaps too often expiate by the loss of life and property, but seldom urge them to the abjuration of a religion, the loss of whose privileges deprives the wretched apostate of every human good! It is by a previous cultivation of their moral powers, we may hope to influence their religious belief; it is by teaching them to love us, that we can lead them to listen to us; it is by inspiring them with respect for our virtues, that we can give them a confidence in our doctrine: but this has not always been the system adopted by European reformers, and the religion we proffer them is seldom illustrated by its influence on our own lives. We bring them a spiritual creed, which commands them to forget the world, and we take from them temporal possessions, which prove how much *we live for it*."

"With such mildness in opinion, and such tolerance towards the prejudices of others, you have doubtless succeeded in your mission, where a zeal not more pure, but more ardent, would have failed?"

The Missionary changed colour at the observation, and replied—"The zeal of the members of the congregation of the Mission can never be doubted, since they voluntarily devote themselves to the cause of Christianity; yet to effect a change in the religion of sixty millions of people, whose doctrines[11] claim their authority from the records of the most ancient nations,—whose faith is guarded by the pride of rank, the interest of priesthood, by its own abstract nature, by local habits, and confirmed prejudices; a faith which resisted the sword of Mahmoud and the arms of Timur,—requires a power seldom vested in man, and which time, a new order of things in India, and the Divine will, can alone, I believe, accomplish."

"You return then to the centre of your mission without any converts to your exertion and your eloquence?"

"No fruit has been indeed gathered equal to the labour or the hope; for I have made but one proselyte, who purchases the truths of Christianity by the forfeiture of every earthly good!"

"A *Brahmin* perhaps?

"A Brahmin's daughter! the chief priestess of the pagoda of Sirinagar, in Cashmire, a prophetess, and *Brachmachira*; whose conversion may indeed be deemed a miracle!"

"Your neophyte is then that young and beautiful person we first beheld lifeless *in your arms*, in the desert?"

"The same," said the Missionary, again changing colour: "She has already received the rites of baptism, and I am conveying her to *Goa*, there her profession of some holy order may produce, by its example, a salutary effect, which her conversion never could have done in Cashmire; a place where the Brahminical bigotry has reached its zenith, and where her forfeiture of cast would have rendered her an object of opprobrium and

[11] "Notwithstanding the labours of the Missionaries for upwards of two hundred years, out of perhaps one hundred millions of *Hindus*, there are not twelve thousand *Christians*, and those are almost all entirely *chancalas*, or *outcasts*."—*Sketches of the History of the Religion, Learning, and Manners of the Hindus, p.* 48.

aversion!"—As the Missionary spoke, he raised his eyes to the face of the person he addressed; but it was still shaded by the hood of his cloak, yet he met an eye so keen, so malignant in its glance, that, could he have shrunk from any mortal look, he would have shrunk from this. Struck by its singular expression, and by the certainty of having before met it, he remained for many minutes endeavouring to collect his thoughts, and, believing himself justified by the freedom of the stranger's inquiries, to question him as to his country and profession, he turned round to address him: but the strangers had now both moved away, and the Missionary then first observed, that he who had been silent during this short dialogue, and whom he still held in view, was employed in writing on a tablet, as though he noted down the heads of the conversation. This circumstance appeared too strange not to excite some curiosity, and much amazement. The person who addressed him spoke in the Hindu dialect, as it was spoken at *Lahore*; but he believed it possible, that he might have been some emissary from the Jesuits convent there, on his way to the Inquisitorial college at Goa: this for a moment disquieted him; for his mind, long divided by conflicting passions, had lost its wonted self-possession and lofty independence: he had been recently accustomed to suspect himself; and he now feared that his zeal, relaxed by passion, had weakened that severity of principle which once admitted of no innovation, and thought it not impossible that he might have expressed his sentiments with a freedom which bigotry could easily torture into an evidence of heresy itself. He again sought the two strangers, but in vain; for they had joined the advanced troop of the caravan; while a feeling, stronger than any they had excited, still fixed him in the rear, near the mohaffah of Luxima.

The caravan now pursued its toilsome route through the rich and varying district of *Scindi*; and the fresh and scented gales, which blew from the Indian sea, revived the languid spirits of the drooping Neophyte; and gave to her eye and cheek, the beam and glow of health and loveliness. Not so the Missionary:—as he advanced towards the haunts of civilized society, the ties by which he was bound to it, and its influence and power over his opinions and conduct, which a fatal passion, cherished in wilds and deserts, had banished from his mind, now rushed to his recollection with an overwhelming force—he gloomily anticipated the disappointment which awaited his return to Goa; the triumph of his enemies, and the discomfiture of his friends; the inferences which might be drawn from the sex and beauty of his solitary Neophyte; and, above all, the eternal separation from the sole object, that alone had taught him the supreme bliss, which the most profound and precious feeling of nature can bestow,—a separation, imperiously demanded by religion, by honour, and by the respect still due to his character and holy profession. It was his intention to place her in a house of Franciscan Sisters, an order whose purity and mildness was suited to her gentle nature. But, when he remembered the youth and loveliness he was about to entomb, the feelings and affections he was about to sacrifice—the warm, the tender, the impassioned heart he should devote to a cold and gloomy association, with rigid and uncongenial spirits—when he beheld her in fancy ascending the altar steps, resigning, by vows she scarcely understood, the brilliant illusions of her own imposing and fanciful faith, and embracing doctrines to which her mind was not yet familiarized, and against which her strong rooted prejudices and ardent feelings still revolted,—when he beheld her despoiled of those lovely and luxuriant tresses which had so often received the homage of his silent admiration, and almost felt his own hands tremble, as he placed on her brow the veil which concealed her from him for ever,—when he caught the parting sigh,—when his glance died under the expression of those dove-like eyes, which, withdrawing their looks from the cross, would still throw their lingering and languid light upon his receding form!—then, worked up to a frenzy of love and of affection, by the image which his fancy and his feelings had pictured to his heart, he eagerly sought her presence as though the moment was already arrived, when he should lose her love for ever; and he hung, in such despairing fondness round her, that Luxima, touched by the expression of his countenance, sought to know the cause of his agitation, and to soothe his spirits. The Missionary leaned over the vehicle, in which she reposed, to catch the murmurings of her low and tender voice.

"Thou art sad," she said, "and melancholy hangs upon thy brow, now that danger is over, and suffering almost forgotten. Is it only in the midst of perils, which strike death upon weaker souls, that *thine* rejoices? for amidst the conflicts of varying elements, thou wast firm; in the burning desert, thou wast unsubdued—Oh! how often has my fancy likened thee to the great *vesanti* plant, which, when it meets not the mighty stem round which it is its nature to twine and flourish, droops not, though forsaken, but assuming the form and structure of a towering tree, betrays its aspiring origin, and points its lofty branches towards the heavens, whose storms it dares and thus doth thou seem greatest, when most exposed and firmest, when least supported. Oh! father," she added, with an ardour she had long suppressed, "didst thou feel as I feel, one look of love would chase all sorrow from thy heart, and sadness from thy brow."

"But Luxima," returned the Missionary, infected by her impassioned tenderness, as if that were almost love's last look, "if, when every tie was drawn so closely round the heart, that both must break together—if the fatal conciousness of being loved, have become so necessary to existence, that life seems without it, a cold and dreary waste—if under the influence of feelings such as these, the moment of an eternal separation dawns in all its hopeless and insupportable misery on the soul, then every look which love bestows, mingles sadness with affection, and despair with bliss." Luxima turned pale; and she raised her tearful eyes to his face, not daring to inquire, but by look, how far that dreadful moment was yet distant. The Missionary pointed out to her a distant view of Tatta, whence they were to sail for Goa; and, stifling the emotions of the lover, and the feelings of the man, he endeavoured to rally back his fading zeal; he spoke to her only in the language of the Missionary and the Priest; he spoke of resigning her to *God alone*; of that perfect conversion which his absence even *more* than his presence would effect!—he described to her the nature and object of the life she was about to embrace,—its peace—its sanctity—its exemptions from human trials, and human passions—and above all, the eternal beatitude to which it led;—he spoke to her of their separation, as inevitable,—and, concealing the struggles which existed in his own mind, he sought only to soothe, to strengthen, and to tranquillize hers. Luxima heard him in silence: she made neither objections nor reply. He was struck by the sudden change which took place in her countenance, when she learned how soon they were to part, and how inevitable was their separation; it was a look resolute and despairing,—as if she defied the destiny, cruel as it was, which seemed to threaten her. At some distance from Tatta, the ardours of a vertical sun obliged the caravan to halt, and seek a temporary shade amidst the umbrageous foliage of a luxuriant grove, refreshed by innumerable streams, flowing into the Indus.

Luxima left her mohaffah, and, supported by the Missionary, sought those shades, which so strongly recalled to her remembrance, the lovely groves of Cashmire,—and the recollections so sad, and yet so precious, which rushed on her mind, were opposed by those feelings which swelled in her bosom, when a distant view of Tatta recalled to her memory the approach of that hour which was so soon to lead her to Goa, to the destined altar of her immolation!—She reflected on the past—she anticipated the future;—and, for the first time, the powerful emotions of which she was capable, betrayed themselves with a violence almost irreconcilable with her gentle and tender nature.—Convulsed with long-stifled feelings, to which she now gave vent, she bathed the earth whereon she had thrown herself, with tears; and, with an eloquence dictated by love and by despair, she denied the existence of an affection which could voluntarily resign its object;—she upbraided equally her lover and herself; and, amidst expressions of reproach and remorse, was still less penitent than tender,—still less lamented her errors, than the approaching loss of him, for whom she had committed them.

"Thou sayest that I am dear to thee," she said; "and yet I am sacrificed; and by him for whom I have abandoned all, I am now myself abandoned.—Oh! give me back to my country, my peace, my fame; or suffer me still to remain near thee, and I will rejoice in the loss of all.—Thou sayest it is the law of thy religion that thou obeyest, when thou shalt send me from thee:—but, if it is a virtue in thy religion to stifle the best and purest feelings of the heart, that nature implants, how shall I believe in, or adopt, its tenets?—I, whose nature, whose faith itself, was love—how from thee shall I learn to subdue my feelings, who first taught me to substitute a human, for a heavenly passion?—Alas! I have but changed the object, the *devotion* is still the same; and thou art loved by the *outcast*, as the Priestess once loved Heaven only."

"Luxima," returned the Missionary, distracted equally by his own feelings and by hers, "let us from the sufferings we now endure, learn the extent of the weakness and the errors which we thus, be it hoped, so painfully expiate; for, it is by despair, such as now distracts us, that Heaven punishes the unfortunate, who suffers a passionate and exclusive sentiment to take possession of the heart, for a creature frail and dependant as ourselves. Oh! my daughter, had we but listened to the voice of religion, or of reason, as we have hearkened to our own passions, the most insupportable of human afflictions could not now have befallen us; and that pang by which we are agonized, at the brink of eternal separation, would have been spared to those souls, which a divine and imperishable object would then have solely occupied and involved."

"I, at least," said Luxima, firmly, yet with wildness, "I shall not long endure that pang:—Thinkest thou that I shall long survive *his* loss for whom I have sacrificed all? Oh! no; it was *thou* I followed, and not thy doctrines; for, pure and sublime as they may be, they yet came darkly and confusedly to my soul: but the sentiments thy presence awakened in my heart, were not opposed by any previous thought or feelings of my life; they were true to all its natural impulses, and, if not understood, they were *felt* and *answered*; they mingled with my whole being, and now, even now, form an imperishable part of my existence.—Shudder not thus, but pity, and forgive me! nor think that, weak as I am, I will deprive thee of thy triumph:—yes, thou shalt lead to the Christian Temple, the descendant of Brahma! thou shalt offer up, a sacrifice on the Christian altar, the first apostate, drawn from the most illustrious of the Indian casts,—a Prophetess! who for thee abandoned the homage of a Divinity,—a woman, who for thee resisted the splendours of an empire.—And this I will tell to the Christians in the midst of their temple, and their congregation—that they may know the single solitary convert thy powers have made, is more than all the proselytes thy brethen e'er brought to kiss the Cross: this I shall do *less in faith* than *love*; not for *my* sake, but for *thine*.—Yet, oh! be thou near me at the altar of sacrifice; let me cling to thee to the last—for, stern and awful as thy religion is, its severity will not refuse me that: yet, if it punish thee, even for pitying—"

"And, thinkest thou," interrupted the Missionary wildly, "that it is *punishment* I fear, or that if the enjoyment of thy love, fatal and dear as thou art, could be purchased by suffering that I would shrink from its endurance? No! it is not torture the most acute I shun—it is *crime that I abhor*—and, equal to to sustain all sufferings but those of conscience, I now live only in dread of myself! For oh! Luxima, even yet I might spare myself and thee a life so cold, so sad and dreary, that conscious virtue and true religion only can support us through it,—even yet, escaping from every eye, save Heaven's, we might together fly to the pathless wilds of these delicious regions, and live in sinful bliss, the commoners of nature:—But, Luxima, the soul of him who loves, and who resists thee, is formed of such a temper, that it can taste no perfect joy in weakness or in crime. Pity then, and yet respect, him who, loving thee and virtue equally, can ne'er know happiness without nor with thee,—who, thus condemned to suffer, without ceasing, submits not to his fate, but is overpowered by its tyranny, and who, alike helpless and unresigned, opposes while he suffers, and repines while he endures; knowing only the remorse of guilt without its enjoyments, and expecting its retribution, without daring to deprecate its weight." Exhausted and overpowered, he fell prostrate on the earth; cold damps hung on his brow, and burning tears fell from his inflamed eyes.—Luxima, terrified by his emotion, faint and trembling, crept timidly and tenderly towards him; and, pressing his hands, she murmured soothingly, yet with firmness, "Since then we can both only live to suffer or to err, to be miserable or to be guilty, wherefore should we not die?"

The Missionary raised his eyes to her face, and its expression of loveliness and love, though darkened by despair, rendered her more enchanting in his eyes, than she had ever yet appeared: he felt her tears on his hands, which she pressed alternately to her eyes and to her lips; and this eloquent though silent expression of an affection so pure, which he believed was to be the last proof of love he might ever receive, overwhelmed him.

Silent and motionless, he withdrew not his hands from the clasp of hers; he gazed on her with unrestrained feelings of love and pity, his whole soul seeming to diffuse itself through his eyes, over her countenance and figure. It was in this transient moment of high-wrought emotions, that they were suddenly surrounded by a group of persons who sprang from behind a rock. Luxima was torn from the arms, which but now protectingly encircled her; and the Missionary was seized with a violence, that, in the first moment of amazement and horror, deprived him of all presence of mind. But the feeble plaints of Luxima, who was borne away in the arms of one of the assailants, recalled to his bewildered mind a consciousness of their mutual sufferings, and situations:—he struggled with all the strength of frenzy in the strong grasp of the two persons who held him;—he shook them from him as creatures of inferior force and nature; and looked so powerful, in his uncurbed rage, that a third, who stood armed before him, attempted not to arrest his flight, as he sprang forward to the rescue of Luxima, who lay lifeless in the arms of the person who was carrying her away; but in the next moment his own encircled her: the person from whom he had torn her, seemed no less bold, no less resolved than he; drawing a pistol from beneath his robe, he pointed it to the Missionary's breast; and exclaimed, "To resist, is but to increase your crimes, and to endanger your life." The Missionary gently disengaged himself from Luxima, who sunk to the earth, and, springing like a lion on his opponent, he seized his arm;—closely entwined in bonds of mutual destruction, they wrestled for life and death, with a strength almost supernatural,—at last, Hilarion wresting the pistol from the hand of his adversary, flung him against a rock, at whose base he lay apparently without life.—His three associates now came to the scene of action—armed, and with looks that threatened to avenge the fate of their companion; but the Missionary stood firm and unappalled, his eye lowring defiance, and raising Luxima in one arm, while with the other he pointed the pistol towards them, he said boldly, "Whoe'er you be, and whatever may have tempted you to this desperate outrage, I shall not spare the life of him who dares approach one single step."

The persons looked in consternation on each other; but one of them, whose face was till now concealed, threw back his hood and robe, and discovered on his breast, the Badge which distinguishes *the officers of the Inquisition*![12] It was then, that the Missionary recognized in the European traveller the Coadjutor whom he had disgraced and dismissed from his appointment, during their voyage to India. Amazed, confounded, but not subdued, he met, with an undaunted look, the keen, malignant, and avengeful glance, which was now directed at him: "Knowest thou me?" demanded the Inquisitor

[12] "They all wear (the Familiares de Santo Officio), as a mark of creditable distinction, a gold medal, upon which are engraven the Arms of the Inquisition."

Stockdale's History of the Inquisitions.

scoffingly, "who, now high in power in the highest of all human tribunals, was once covered with shame and opprobrium, by thy superior excellence! Where now are all the mighty virtues of the *man without a fault*? where now are the wonders which his zeal and genius promised? what are the fruits of his unrivalled Mission? Behold him! supporting on his bosom, the victim of his seductive arts!—his sacrilegious hand, pointing an instrument of death at those who are engaged in the duties of that holy office, whose censure he has incurred by dreadful heresies, by breach of solemn vows, and by his heretical defamation of a sacred Order!"—While the Inquisitor yet spoke, several persons from the Caravan had arrived on the spot, to witness a scene so singular and so unexpected: Luxima too, who had recovered her senses, still trembling and horror-struck, clung to the bosom, which now so wildly heaved to the emotions of rage and indignation.

Silent for many minutes, the Missionary stood gazing with a look of proud defiance and ineffable contempt upon his avengeful enemy: "And know *you* not me?" he at last exclaimed, with a lofty scorn—"you knew me once, supreme, where *you* dared not *soar*!—Such as *I then was*, such *I now am*; in every thing unchanged—and still, in every thing, *your* superior!—Grovelling and miserable *as you are* even in your unmerited elevation—this you *still* feel;—speak, then; what are your orders!—tremble not, but declare them!—It is the Count of Acugna, it is the Apostolic *Nuncio* of *India*, who commands you!"—Pale with stifled rage, the Inquisitor drew from his bosom the brief, by which he was empowered to call those before the Inquisitorial Court, whose conduct and whose opinions should fall under the suspicions of those emissaries, which it had deputed to visit the Christian establishments in the interior of India.—The Missionary glanced his eye over the awful instrument, and bowed low to the Red Cross imprinted at its head: the Inquisitor then said, "Hilarion, of the Order of St. Francis, and member of the Congregation of the Mission;—I arrest you in the name of the Holy Office, and in presence of these its ministers, that you may answer to such charges as I shall bring against you, before *the tribunal* of the Inquisition." At these words, the Missionary turned pale!—nature stood checked by religion!—passion submitted to opinion, and prejudice governed those *feelings*, over which *reason* had lost all sway. He let fall the instrument of death, which he had held in his hand till now; the voice of the

Church had addressed him, and all the powerful force of his religious habits returned upon his soul: he, who till now had felt only as a *man*, remembered he was a *religious*; he who had long, who had so recently, acknowledged the precious influence of human feeling, now recalled to mind that he had vowed the sacrifice of *all* human feeling to Heaven!—and he who had resisted oppression, and avenged insult, now recollected, that by the religion he professed, he was bound when one *cheek was smitten, to turn the other*.

The rage which had blazed in the eyes of the indignant, the blood which had boiled in the veins of the brave, no longer flashed in the glance, or crimsoned the cheek of the Christian Missionary; yet still it was—

> "Awe from above, that quelled his heart, nought else dismayed."

The officers of the Inquisition now approached, to bind his arms, and to lead him away; but Luxima, with a shriek of horror, threw herself between them, ignorant of the nature of the danger which assailed her lover and her friend, and believing it nothing less than death itself: her wild and frenzied supplications, her beauty and affection, touched the hearts of those who surrounded them. The Missionary had already excited a powerful interest in his favour: the popular feeling is always on the side of resistance against oppression—for men, however vicious individually, are generally virtuous in the mass: his fellow-travellers, therefore, boldly advanced, to rescue one, whose air and manner had captivated their imaginations. The passions of a multitude know no precise limit; the partisans of the Missionary only waited for the orders of him whom they were about to avenge: they said, "Shall we throw those men under the camels feet? or shall we bind them to those rocks, and leave them to their fate?"

The Europeans shuddered, and turned pale!

The Missionary cast on them a glance of contempt and pity, and, looking round him with an air at once dignified and grateful, he said, "My friends, my heart is deeply touched by your generous sympathy; good and brave men ever unite, of whatever region, or whatever faith they may be: but I belong to a religion whose spirit it is to save, and not to destroy; suffer then, these men to live; they are but the agents of a higher power, whose scrutiny they challenge me to meet.—I go to appear before that tribunal of that church, whose voice is my law, and from which a Christian minister can make no appeal,—I trust I go to contend *best* with the *best*; prepared rather to suffer death myself, than to cause the death of others."

Then turning to the Inquisitor he said, pointing to Luxima, whom he again supported in his arms, "Remember, that by a word I could have had you mingled with the dust I tread on; but, as you prize that life I have preserved, guard and protect this sacred, this consecrated vestal!—*look at her!*—otherwise than pure and innocent, you dare not believe her: know then, also, she is a Christian Neophyte, who has received the Baptismal rites, and who is destined to set a bright example to her idolatrous nation, and to become the future spouse of God."

Subdued and mortified, the officers of the Inquisition made no reply. He whom the Missionary had wounded, now crawled towards the others—they surrounded their unresisting prisoner, who bore along the feeble form of the Indian: silent, and weeping, she was consigned to the mohaffah she had before occupied; and, the Missionary having ascended the back of his camel, the caravan was again in motion—two of the Inquisitors remained with their prisoner—the other two had rode on before the caravan to *Tatta*.

Chapter XVI.

IT was night when the travellers reached the suburbs of the ancient city of Tatta; the caravan had been lessened of its numbers during its progress; those who remained, now dispersed in various directions: the Inquisitors, instead of proceeding with their charge to a *Caravansera*, carried him and the Neophyte to a small fortress which belonged to a Spanish garrison; a guard of soldiers, headed by the two Inquisitors, who had preceded the caravan, received them at its portals.

The Missionary guessed his fate,—dreadful as it was, he met it not unprepared: he saw himself surrounded by an armed force; he knew that, were he inclined to offer it, all resistance would be vain; and he submitted, with all the grandeur of human dignity, with all the firmness of religious fortitude, to a destiny now inevitable.

But Luxima still clung to him: the gloomy air of all around her, the fierce looks of the soldiers, their arms glittering to the dusky light of a solitary lamp, which hung suspended in the centre of a vast and desolate guardroom; the black cowls and scowling countenances of the Inquisitors, all struck terror on the timid soul of the Indian. She cast round a fearful and terrified glance, and would then have sunk upon the bosom of her sole protector and friend on earth, but, exposed as they were to the observation of their persecutors, the Missionary, for her sake even more than for his own, rejected the impulse of his feelings, and, turning away his head to conceal the agony of his countenance, he held her from him.—It was then that the heart of Luxima, sinking within her bosom, seemed to have received its death wound;—she fixed her closing eyes on him, who thus almost seemed to resign her to misery and to suffering, unsupported and unpitied—but she wept not, and one of the Inquisitors bore her away, unresisting, and almost lifeless, in his arms. An exclamation of horror burst from the lips of the Missionary; and, with an involuntary motion, he advanced a few steps to follow her; betraying, in his wild and haggard looks, the feelings by which his soul was torn. But the guards interposed—he could not even himself desire, that she might remain with him; and the Inquisitor, fixing his eyes on his agitated countenance, with a look of scoffing malignancy, said: "Fear not for your concubine, she shall be taken care of."—At these words, a deep scarlet suffused the cheek of the Missionary; fire flashed from his dark rolling eye, and he cast a look on his insulting oppressor, so blasting in its glance, that he seemed to wither beneath its terrific influence.—"Observe!" he said, with a voice of thunder, "I repeat it to you, it is a Christian Neophyte, pure, spotless, and unsullied, which you have now taken under your protection; look therefore that you consider her as such, as you shall answer it to that God, to whom she is about to consecrate her sinless life; as you shall answer it to that Church, whose ministers you are.—Be this remembered by you as priests; as *men*, forget not *she is a woman*!" Then, turning to his guards, he said with haughtiness, "Lead on;"—as though he still commanded, even in obeying; and he was immediately led to a tower in a remote part of the fortress.

The members of the Inquisitorial Court, into whose power a singular coincidence of circumstances had thrown the Missionary, were returning from visiting the Christian institution at Lahore, of whose abuses and disorders the grand Inquisitor had received secret intelligence, when the chief of the party, who had been raised to his present dignity by the low arts of cunning and duplicity, discovered in the supposed lover of a fugitive Indian, that once infallible man, of whose rigid virtue, and severe unbending justice, he had been the victim; conscious, that in detecting and exposing the frailty of one who had "bought golden opinions, from all sorts of persons," he should, while he gratified his own private vengeance, present a grateful victim to the Jesuits and Dominicans, who equally hated the Franciscan, for his order, his popularity, and his unrivalled genius,—he soon sought and found sufficient grounds of accusation, to lay the basis of his future ruin. With an artifice truly jesuitical, he drew the Missionary into a conversation, which he obliged one of his brethren to listen to, and note down; and, from the freedom of those religious opinions he had induced the Missionary to discuss, and from the tender nature of the ties which seemed to exist between him and his lovely associate,—Heresy, and the seduction of a Neophyte, were the crimes to be alleged against a man, whose disgrace was destined to be commensurate to the splendour of his triumphs.

On the day following their arrival at Tatta, the Missionary was conveyed on board a Spanish vessel, which lay in the Indus, and was bound for Goa. On his way he passed the *litter* which Luxima, he believed, occupied; but it was closely covered. He shuddered, and for a moment the heroism of virtue deserted him—he doubted not that she would be conveyed in the same vessel with him to Goa; and, as he knew that supplication would be fruitless, and that in humbling himself to intreaty he would not effect the purpose for which he stooped, he made no effort to obtain an interview with her: he believed too that the insatiable desire of the Jesuits for conversion would render her safety and preservation an object to them; and that she would owe to the bigotry of their zeal, that mercy which she could not expect from the suggestions of their humanity—but that he should never again behold her, the object of his only love, the companion of his wandering, and the partner of his sufferings, was an idea dictated by despair, from which religion withdrew her light, and hope her solace. Placed in a close and unwholesome confinement, it was in vain he sought to catch the sound of Luxima's voice; it was in vain he hazarded an inquiry relative to her situation: silence and mystery still surrounded him; no beam shone upon the darkness of his days; no answer was returned to his inquiries; no pity was given to his sufferings; all was dreary hopeless gloom! all was the loss of fame, the loss of love! of all that the high ambition of piety had promised! of all that the exquisite feelings of nature had bestowed!—Still pursued "by thoughts of lost happiness and lasting shame," and joined only in *equal ruin* with her for whom he had encountered misery and affliction, and on whose innocent head he had heaped it,—he now saw that the sufferings of man resulted less from the constitution of his nature, than from the obstinacy with which he abandons the dictates of Providence, and devotes himself to those illusions which the law of human reason, and the impulse of human affection, equally oppose. He remembered the feelings with which the

Brahmin Priestess and the Christian Missionary had first mutually met; he contrasted their first interview with their present situations, alike as they now were *the victims of mistaken* zeal; and he accused that misconstruction of the laws of Providence, those false distinctions, which superstition has erected between the species, as the source of the severest sufferings to which mankind was condemned. For himself, he had no hope: he knew the character of his judges, the sentiments they bore in general to his order, and in particular to him; he knew the influence of the tribunal at which they presided, he knew that those whom they intended to destroy, no human power could preserve. But while he accused himself of relaxation in his zeal, of negligence in his mission, of suffering a guilty passion to subdue the force of his mind, and the influence of his religion, he believed his enemies to be but the blind agents of that Heaven, whose wrath he had justly provoked; for, still bringing his new-born feelings to the test of his ancient opinions, he continued to oppose religion to nature, and deemed himself sunk in guilt, because he had not risen above humanity.

It was on a day bright and sunny as that on which the Apostolic Nuncio left *Goa* in all the triumph of superior and unrivalled excellence that he returned to it a *prisoner* and in *chains*. His enemies had determined that his disgrace should be as striking and as public as his triumph; that the idol of the people should be dashed before their eyes from the shrine erected to his glory; and that envy and bigotry, under the guise of religion and justice should gratify the insatiate spirit of persecution and vengeance. Before the illustrious criminal was permitted to land the intelligence of his return under circumstances so different from those his departure had promised, and dark inuendos of the nature and extent of his fault, were artfully circulated through *Goa*, till the public mind, soured by the disappointments of its hopes and its confidence, was prepared to receive the Nuncio with a contempt equal to the admiration it formerly bestowed on him. At last a guard of Spanish soldiers, accompanied by the officers of the Holy Office, were sent to conduct him to the prison of the Inquisition. A multitude of persons had assembled to see him pass; but they no longer beheld the same creature whom they had last so loudly greeted with acclamations of reverential homage, and on whose mild and majestic brow passion had impressed no trace, whose commanding eye was brightened by holy joy, and whose life of sinless purity was marked in the seraphic character of his inspired countenance! His person was now almost as changed as his fate: it was worn away by suffering, by fatigue, by internal conflicts, and faded by its exposure to the varying clime; the experience of human frailty in himself, and of human turpitude in others, marked his brow with traces of distrust and disappointment;—his enthusiasm was fled! his zeal subdued by the fatal consequences of its unsuccessful efforts! and love, and affliction, and shame, and indignation, the opprobrium he endured, and the innocence he could not establish; the injustice under which he laboured, and the malignity he despised—all mingled their conflicts in his soul, all shed over his air and look the sullen grandeur of a proud despair, superior to complaint, and inaccessible to hope; yet "not all *lost* in *loss* itself," gleams of his mind's untarnished glory still brightened at intervals his look of gloom—and, still appearing little less than "archangel ruined," he proceeded, manacled, but lofty and towering above the guards who surrounded him. An awful silence reigned on every side; and even those who deemed him culpable, saw him so mighty in *his fall*, that while they accused him of guilt, they believed him superior to weakness; respecting while they condemned, and admiring while they pitied him. As a member of the noble house of *Acugna*, whatever were the charges brought against him, he could not fail to excite interest in Goa, where the Portuguese were coalesced by a common feeling of suffering under the oppression of the Spanish government: but the terrors which surrounded the most dreadful of all human tribunals; a tribunal which was seconded, in the hierarchy of Goa, by all the influence of civil authority; its being invested with the power of life and death, and superstitiously believed even with that of salvation itself, awed the boldest heart, and alike silenced the feelings of patriotism, and stilled the impulse of humanity! Not even a murmur of resistance was heard; the accused and his guards passed silently on to the prison of the Holy Office; they reached its gloomy court; the portals closed upon the victim, and the light of hope was shut out for ever!

No breath transpired of the dark mysterious deeds which passed within the mansion of horror and superstition; and its awful investigations were conducted with a secresy which baffled all inquiry:[13] the impenetrable

[13] The people also dare not speak of this Inquisition, but with the utmost respect

cloud which hung over the fate of the Missionary, could only be cleared up when that dreaded day arrived, upon which the dungeons of the Inquisition were to yield up their tenants to punishment, to liberty, or—to death!

At this period a sullen gloom hung over the city of Goa, resembling the brooding of a distant storm:—it was rumoured, that the power of the Spanish government in Portugal and its colonies was on the point of extinction, and it was known by many fatal symptoms, that the Indians were ripe for insurrection. The arts used by the Dominicans and the Jesuits for the conversion of the followers of Brahma, the evil consequences which had arisen by forfeiture of cast, (for many families had shared the ignominy heaped on the devoted head of the individual apostate) with the coercive tyranny of the Spanish government, had excited in the breasts of the mild, patient, and long-enduring Hindus, a principle of resistance, which waited only for some strong and sudden impulse to call it into action[14]; and it was observed that this disposition had particularly betrayed itself on a recent and singular occasion.

A woman who bore on her forehead the mark of a descendant of Bramah (the sacred *tellertum*), and round her neck the sacrificial threads or *dsandam* of their tutelar god, was seen to enter a convent of Dominican nuns, led by an officer of the Inquisition, and surrounded by Dominican and *Jesuit priests*! The faded beauty of her perfect form, her noble and distinguished air, the agony of her countenance, and the silent tears which fell from her eyes when she turned them on those of her own cast and country, who stood near the litter from which she alighted, awakened a strong and powerful emotion in their feelings; and it was not decreased, when a Cashmirian, who was present, declared that the said apostate was Luxima, the Brahmachira

---

and reverence; and if by accident the slightest word should escape one, which concerned it ever so little, it would be necessary immediately to accuse and inform against one's self. People are frequently confined to the prison for one, two, or three years, without knowing the reason, and are visited only by officers of the Inquisition, and never suffered to behold any other person.—*History of the Inquisition by Stockdale*, p. 213.

[14] An insurrection of a fatal consequence took place in *Vellore* so late as 1806, and a mutiny at Nundydrag and Benglore, occurred about the same period: both were supposed to have originated in the religious bigotry of the natives, suddenly kindled by the supposed threatened violation of their faith from the Christian settlers.

and prophetess of Cashmire. The person who industriously circulated this intelligence, was the *pundit* of Lahore, the preceptor of the Missionary. His restless and unsettled spirit had led him to Goa: some imprudent and severe observations which he had let fall against the Inquisitorial power, had nearly proved his destruction, but his talents had extricated him; he had engaged as secretary and interpreter to the Spanish Viceroy, and obtained his favour and protection by those arts of conciliation, of which he was so perfectly the master. His hatred of the Inquisition and his love of intrigue and of commotion, which gave play to the finesse of his genius, and the activity of his mind, led him to seize every opportunity of exciting his compatriots to resist the European power in Goa; and it was about this period that the arrival of Luxima furnished him with an event favourable to his views. He had in vain sought to attract her attention on her way to the Convent of the Dominicans; nor until her arrival at its portal had he succeeded in catching her eye; he then effected it by dropping his muntras at her feet. Absorbed as she appeared to be, this little incident did not escape her attention: she raised her tear-swollen eyes to his, with a look of sudden recognition, for she had known him in the days of her glory; but the Cashmirian, with an almost imperceptible motion of his finger across his lips, implying silence, carelessly picked up his beads and passed on, as the doors of the Christian sanctuary shut out from the eyes of the multitude the priestess of Brahma.

It was on the eve of St. Jago de Compostello, that the usually tranquil abode of the Dominican sisters exhibited a scene of general consternation: the *Indian Catechuman*, committed to their pious care, had mysteriously disappeared a few days after her reception into their Order. Her conduct had not prepared them for an event so extraordinary from her: either unable or unwilling to speak their language, they had not once heard the sound of her voice, save that at sun-set she sung a few low wild notes, through the bars of the casement of her cell, which the younger nuns delighted to catch in the garden beneath, believing that the day was not distant, when a voice so angelic would blend its melody with the holy strains of the Christian choir; but she appeared in every other respect docile, unresisting, and timid almost to wildness. She had suffered them to exchange her Indian dress for the habit of a novice of St. Dominick; she had unreluctantly accompanied them to their church, and assisted at their devotions: her looks were indeed wandering and wild, and seemingly always sent in search of some particular object; but she made no inquiry, she uttered no complaint, and the secret disorder of her mind was only visible in her countenance; which wore the general expression of confirmed melancholy, the sadness of unutterable affliction. A meekness so saintly, a gentleness so seraphic, excited hopes in the breast of the abbess and the sisterhood, which were suddenly destroyed by the miraculous disappearance of the Catechuman. The convent grounds, the gardens of the Viceroy, which were only divided from them by a low wall, were vainly searched; and no circumstance attending her flight could be ascertained, but that she had escaped by the casement of her cell; one of the bars of which had been removed from the brick-work. The *Provincial* of the Order having been made acquainted with the event, which was placed to the account of *pagan sorcery*, an order was issued from the Holy Office, offering a reward to whoever should give up the *relapsed infidel*, and threatening death to those who should conceal her; but week after week elapsed, and no one came forward to claim the recompense, or to avert the punishment. The pagan sorceress was no where to be heard of.[15]

[15] The Pagans and Moors of Goa are not subject to the Inquisition till they have been baptized. A disgusting and absurd cruelty is displayed in its treatment of those unfortunate Indians who are accused of magic and sorcery, and, as guilty of such offences, are committed to the flames.—*See Hist. of the Inquisition, p. 243.*

Chapter XVII.

HOWEVER a propensity to evil may be inherent in human nature, it is impossible to conceive an idea of abstract wickedness, uninfluenced by some powerful passion, and existing without any decided reference to some object we wish to attain, or some obstacle we desire to vanquish.

The Pundit of Lahore had seen the Christian Missionary dragged in chains to the dungeon of the Inquisition, and the Priestess of Cashmire delivered up to the tyranny of a fanaticism no less dreadful in the exercise of its power than that from which she had escaped. He considered himself as the remote cause of their mutual sufferings: equally incredulous as to the truth or influence of their respective doctrines, when opposed to the feelings of nature, he had felt a kind of triumph in putting their boasted infallibility to the test, which deserted him the moment he discovered the fatal consequences which arose from the success of his design. Unprincipled and corrupt to a certain degree, when a dereliction from right favoured the views of his interests, or established the justness of his opinions, (for the human mind, whether it credulously bends to imposition, or boldly resists in scepticism, can never wholly relinquish the intolerance of self-love,) he was yet naturally humane and benevolent; and the moment he discovered the fate which awaited the Missionary and his proselyte, he determined to use every exertion to avert it.

Free at all times of admittance to the Viceroy's gardens, he continued to wander incessantly beneath the wall which divided them from the grounds of the convent. He had caught a few notes of Luxima's vesper song, and recognized the air of an Indian hymn, sung upon certain festivals by the priestesses of *Brahma*; he ventured therefore to scale the wall, veiled by the obscurity of a dark night; and by means of a ladder of ropes, he finally effected the escape of the Neophyte: he conveyed her to his own lodging in a retired part of the city, and gave her up to the care of a Jewess, who lived with him, and who, though outwardly professing Christianity from fear and policy, hated equally the Christians and the Pagans; love, however, secured her fealty to her protector, to whom she was ardently devoted; and pity secured her fidelity to the trust he had committed to her care; for the unfortunate Indian was now alike condemned by the religion of truth and the superstition of error—driven with shame and obloquy from the altar of Brahma, her life had become forfeit by the laws of the Inquisition as a relapsed Christian.[16] It was from the order issued from the Holy Office that the Pundit learned the latter circumstances. It was from the lips of the apostate that he learned she had forfeited cast, according to all the awful rites of Braminical excommunication. It was therefore impossible to restore her to her own cast, and difficult to preserve her from the power of her new religion; and he found with regret and dismay, that the efforts he had made to save her, might but ultimately tend to her destruction;—he now considered that his life was involved in hers, and that his own preservation depended upon her concealment. His first thought was to remove her from Goa: but the disorder of her mind had fallen upon her constitution, and she was seized with the *mordechi*[17]—that disease so melancholy, and so dangerous, in those burning climes, where exercise, the sole preventive, is impossible. The ill success of his endeavours hitherto, the impossibility of gaining admittance into the interior of the Santa Casa, destroyed the hopes and checked the intentions of the Pundit, which pointed to the liberation of the Missionary; and the mystery which hung over the fate of a man for whom all Goa was interested, no human power could fathom. But the festival upon which the next *auto da fè* was to be celebrated was fast approaching; and the result of those trials, the accused had sustained at the *messa di santo officio*, could at that period only be ascertained.

---

[16] The Inquisition, which punishes with death relapsed Christians, never inflicts any capital punishment on those who have not received the rites of baptism.—*History of the Inquisition, p. 214.*

[17] A species of delirious fever.

The day had already passed, upon which the ministers of the Inquisition, preceded by their banners, marched from the palace of the Holy Office to the *Campo Santo*, or place of execution, and there by sound of trumpet proclaimed the day and hour on which the *solemn act* of faith was to be celebrated.

That awful day at length arrived—its dawn, that beamed so fearfully to many, was ushered in by the deep toll of the great bell of the Cathedral; a multitude of persons, of every age and sex, Christians, Pagans, Jews, and Mussulmen, filled the streets, and occupied the roofs, the balconies and windows of the houses, to see the procession pass through the principal parts of the city. The awful ceremony at length commenced—the procession was led by the Dominicans, bearing before them a white cross; the scarlet standard of the Inquisition, on which the image of the founder was represented armed with a sword, preceded a band of the *familiars of the Holy Office*, dressed in black robes, the last of whom bore a green cross, covered with black crape; six penitents of the *San Benito* who had escaped death, and were to be sent to the galleys, each conducted by a familiar, bearing the standard of St. Andrew, succeeded, and were followed by the penitents of the *Fuego Revolto*, habited in grey scapulars, painted with reversed flames; then followed some persons bearing the effigies of those who had died in prison, and whose bones were also borne in coffins; the victims condemned to death appeared the last of the awful train; they were preceded by the *Alcaid* of the Inquisition, each accompanied on either side by two officers of the Holy Office, and followed by an officiating priest: a corps of *Halberdeens*, or guards of the Inquisition, closed the procession. In this order it reached the church of St. Dominick, destined for the celebration of *the act of faith*. On either side of the great altar, which was covered with black cloth, were erected two thrones; that on the right was occupied by the Grand Inquisitor; that on the left by the Viceroy and his court: each person having assumed the place destined for him, two Dominicans ascended a pulpit, and read aloud, alternately, the sentences of the guilty, the nature of their crimes, and the species of punishment to which they were condemned. While this awful ceremony took place, each unfortunate, as his sentence was pronounced, was led to the foot of the altar by the Alcaid, where he knelt to receive it. Last of this melancholy band, appeared the *Apostolic Nuncio of India*. Hitherto no torture had forced from him a confession of crimes of which he was guiltless; but the power of his enemies had prevailed, and his innocence was not proof against the testimony of his interested accusers. Summoned to approach the altar, he advanced with the dignity of a self-devoted martyr to receive his sentence; firm alike in look and motion, as though created thing "nought valued he or shunned," he knew his doom to be irrevocable, and met it unappalled.

Man was now to him an atom, and earth a speck! the collective force of his mind was directed to *one sole* object, but that object was—*eternity!* The struggle between the mortal and immortal being was over; passion no longer gave to his imagination the vision of its disappointed desires, nor love the seductive images of its frail enjoyment: the ambition of religious zeal, and the blandishments of tender emotion, no longer influenced a soul which was, in so short a space of time, to be summoned before the tribunal of its God.

Less awed than aweful, he stood at the foot of the judgment seat of his earthly umpire, and heard unshrinking and unmoved his accusation publicly pronounced; but when to the sin of heresy, and breach of monastic vow, was added the *seduction of a Neophyte*, then *nature* for a moment asserted her rights, and claimed the revival of her almost extinguished power—his spirit again descended to earth, his heart with a resistless impulsion opened to the influence of human feeling! to the recollection of human ties! and Luxima, even at the altar's feet, rushed to his memory in all her loveliness, and all her affliction; innocent and persecuted, abandoned and despairing: then, the firmness of his look and mind alike deserted him—his countenance became convulsed—his frame shook—an agonizing solicitude for the hapless cause of his death disputed with Heaven the last thoughts of his life—and his head dropped upon the missal on which his hand was spread according to the form of the ceremony:—but when closely following the enumeration of his crimes, he heard pronounced the aweful sentence of a dreadful and *an immediate death*, then the inspired fortitude of the martyr re-called the wandering feelings of the man, steadied the vibration of nerves, which love, for the last time, had taught to thrill, strengthened the weakness of the fainting heart, and restored to the troubled spirit the soothing peace of holy resignation and religious hope.

The fate of those condemned to the flames was at last announced—the officers of the secular tribunal came forward to seize the victims of a cruel and inexorable bigotry; and the procession increased by the Viceroy, and the Grand Inquisitor, with their respective courts, proceeded to the place of execution.—It was a square, one side of which opened to the sea; the three others were composed of the houses of the Spanish grandees, before which a covered platform was erected, for the *Grand Inquisitor* and the Viceroy; in the centre of the square, three piles of faggots were erected, at a certain distance from each other, one of which was already slowly kindling; the air was still, and breathed the balmy softness of an eastern evening; the sun, something shorn of his beams, was setting in mild glory, and threw a saffron hue on the luxuriant woods which skirt the beautiful bay of Goa—not a ripple disturbed the bosom of the deep; every thing in the natural scene declared the beneficent intentions of the Deity, every thing in the human spectacle declared the perversion of man from the decrees of his Creator. It was on such an evening as this, that the Indian Priestess witnessed the dreadful act of her excommunication; the heavens smiled then, as now; and man, the minister of error, was then, as now, cruel and unjust,—substituting malevolence for mercy, and the horrors of a fanatical superstition for the blessed peace and loving kindness of true religion.

The secular judges had already taken their seats on the platform; the Grand Inquisitor and the Viceroy had placed themselves beneath their respective canopies; the persons who composed the procession were ranged according to their offices and orders,—all but the three unhappy persons condemned to death; they alone were led into the centre of the square, each accompanied by a familiar of the Inquisition, and a confessor. The condemned consisted of two relapsed Indians, and *the Apostolic Nuncio* of *India*. The pile designed for him, was distinguished by a *standard*[18] on which, as was the custom in such cases, an inscription was written, intimating, "that he was to be burnt as a *convicted Heretic who refused to confess his crime*!"

---

[18] "Morreo queimado por hereje convitto negativo."

The timid Indians, who, in the zeal and enthusiasm of their own religion, might have joyously and voluntarily sought the death, they now met with horror, hung back, shuddering and weeping in agony and despair, endeavouring to defer their inevitable sufferings by uttering incoherent prayers and useless supplications to the priests who attended them. The Christian Missionary, who it was intended should suffer first, alone walked firmly up to the pile, and while the martyr light flashed on his countenance, he read unmoved the inscription imprinted on the standard of death; which was so soon to wave over his ashes—then, withdrawing a little on one side, he knelt at the feet of his confessor; the last appeal from earth to heaven was now made; he arose with a serene look; the officers of the bow-string advanced to lead him towards the pile: the silence which belongs to death, reigned on every side; thousands of persons were present; yet the melancholy breeze that swept, at intervals, over the ocean, and died away in sighs, was distinctly heard. Nature was touched on the master-spring of emotion, and betrayed in the looks of the multitude, feelings of horror, of pity, and of admiration, which the bigoted vigilance of an inhuman zeal would in vain have sought to suppress.

In this aweful interval, while the presiding officers of death were preparing to bind their victim to the stake, a form scarcely human, darting with the velocity of lightning through the multitude, reached the foot of the pile, and stood before it, in a grand and aspiring attitude; the deep red flame of the slowly kindling fire shone through a transparent drapery which flowed in loose folds from the bosom of the seeming vision, and tinged with golden hues, those long dishevelled tresses, which streamed like the rays of a meteor on the air;—thus bright and aerial as it stood, it looked like a spirit sent from Heaven in the aweful moment of dissolution to cheer and to convey to the regions of the blessed, the soul which would soon arise, pure from the ordeal of earthly suffering.

The sudden appearance of the singular phantom struck the imagination of the credulous and awed multitude with superstitious wonder.—Even the ministers of death stood for a moment, suspended in the execution of their dreadful office. The Christians fixed their eyes upon the *cross*, which glittered on a bosom whose beauty scarcely seemed of mortal mould, and deemed themselves the witnesses of a miracle, wrought for the salvation of a persecuted martyr, whose innocence was asserted by the firmness and fortitude with which he met a dreadful death.

The Hindoos gazed upon the sacred impress of *Brahma*, marked on the brow of his consecrated offspring; and beheld the fancied *herald* of the tenth *Avater*, announcing vengeance to the enemies of their religion. The condemned victim, still confined in the grasp of the officers of the bow-string, with eyes starting from their sockets, saw only the *unfortunate* he had made—the creature he adored—his disciple!—his mistress!—the Pagan priestess—the Christian Neophyte—his still lovely, though much changed Luxima. A cry of despair escaped from his bursting heart; and in the madness of the moment, he uttered aloud her name. Luxima, whose eyes and hands had been hitherto raised to Heaven, while she murmured the *Gayatra*, pronounced by the Indian women before their voluntary immolation, now looked wildly round her, and, catching a glimpse of the Missionary's figure, through the waving of the flames, behind which he struggled in the hands of his guards, she shrieked, and in a voice scarcely human, exclaimed, "My beloved, I come!—*Brahma* receive and eternally unite our spirits!"—She sprang upon the pile: the fire, which had only kindled in that point where she stood, caught the light drapery of her robe—a dreadful death assailed her—the multitude shouted in horrid frenzy—the Missionary rushed forward—no force opposed to it, could resist the energy of madness, which nerved his powerful arm—he snatched the victim from a fate he sought not himself to avoid—he held her to his heart—the flames of her robe were extinguished in his close embrace;—he looked round him with a dignified and triumphant air—the officers of the Inquisition, called on by their superiors, who now descended from the platforms, sprang forward to seize him:—for a moment, the timid multitude were *still* as the pause of a brooding storm.—Luxima clung round the neck of her deliverer—the Missionary, with a supernatural strength, warded off the efforts of those who would have torn her from him—the hand of fanaticism, impatient for its victim, aimed a dagger at his heart; its point was received in the bosom of the Indian;—she shrieked,—and called upon "Brahma!"—Brahma! Brahma! was re-echoed on every side. A sudden impulse was given to feelings long suppressed:—the timid spirits of the Hindoos rallied to an event which touched their hearts, and roused them from their lethargy of despair;—the sufferings, the oppression they had so long endured, seemed now epitomized before their eyes, in the person of their celebrated and distinguished Prophetess—they believed it was their god who addressed them from her lips—they rushed forward with a hideous cry, to rescue his priestess—and to avenge the long slighted cause of their religion, and their freedom;—they fell with fury on the Christians, they rushed upon the cowardly guards of the Inquisition, who let fall their arms, and fled in dismay.

Their religious enthusiasm kindling their human passions, their rage became at once inflamed and sanctified by their superstitious zeal. Some seized the prostrate arms of the fugitives, others dealt round a rapid destruction by fire; they scattered the blazing faggots, and, snatching the burning brands from the pile, they set on fire the light materials of which the balconies, the verandahs, and platforms were composed, till all appeared one horrid and entire conflagration. The Spanish soldiers now came rushing down from the garrison upon the insurgents,—the native troops, almost in the same moment, joined their compatriots—the engagement became fierce and general—a promiscuous carnage ensued—the Spaniards fought as mercenaries, with skill and coolness; the Indians as enthusiasts, for their religion and their liberty, with an uncurbed impetuosity; the conflict was long and unequal; the Hindoos were defeated; but the Christians purchased the victory of the day by losses which almost rendered their conquest a defeat.

Conclusion.

IN the multitude who witnessed the aweful ceremony of the *auto da fè*, in the church of St. Dominick, stood the Pundit of Lahore; and he heard with horror the sentence of death pronounced against the Christian Missionary. Considering himself as the remote cause of his destruction, he was overwhelmed by compassion and remorse—aware of the ripeness of the Indians to a revolt, he determined on exciting them to a rescue of their compatriots at the place of execution; he knew them prompt to receive every impression which came through the medium of their senses, and connected with the popular prejudices of their religion; when he beheld them following, with sullen looks, the slow march of the procession, to witness the execution of their countrymen, whom they conceived by their obstinate abjuration of the Christian religion to have been seduced from their ancient faith, his hopes strengthened, he moved rapidly among them, exciting the pity of some, the horror of others, and a principle of resistance in all: but it was to an unforeseen accident that he owed the success of his hazardous efforts.

Of the disorder by which Luxima had been attacked, a slight delirium only remained; her health was restored, but her mind was wandering and unsettled; the most affecting species of mental derangement had seized her imagination—the melancholy insanity of sorrow: she wept no tears, she heaved no sighs—she sat still and motionless, sometimes murmuring a Braminical hymn, sometimes a Christian prayer—sometimes talking of her grandsire, sometimes of her lover—alternately gazing on the muntras she had received from one, and the cross that had been given her by the other.

On the day of the *auto da fè*, she sat, as was her custom since her recovery, behind the gauze blind of the casement of the little apartment in which she was confined; she beheld the procession moving beneath it with a fixed and vacant eye, until a form presented itself before her, which struck like light from heaven on her darkened mind; she beheld the friend of her soul; love and reason returned together; intelligence revived to the influence of affection—she felt, and thought, and acted—whatever were his fate, she resolved to share it:—she was alone, her door was not fastened, she passed it unobserved, she darted through the little vestibule which opened to the street; the procession had turned into another, but the street was still crowded—so much so, that even her singular appearance was unobserved; terrified and bewildered, she flew down an avenue that led to the sea, either because it was empty and silent, or that her reason was again lost, and she was unconscious whither she went, till chance brought her into the "square of execution!"—she saw the smoke of the piles rising above the heads of the multitude—in every thing she beheld, she saw a spectacle similar to that which the self-immolation of the Brahmin women presents:—the images thus presented to her disordered mind, produced a natural illusion—she believed the hour of her sacrifice and her triumph was arrived, that she was on the point of being united in heaven to him whom she had alone loved on earth; and when she heard her name pronounced by his well-known voice, she rushed to the pile in all the enthusiasm of love and of devotion. The effect produced by this singular event was such as, under the existing feelings of the multitude, might have been expected. During the whole of the tumult, the Pundit did not for a moment lose sight of the Missionary, who, still clasping Luxima in his arms, was struggling with her through the ranks of destruction; the Pundit approaching him, seized his arm, and, while all was uproar and confusion, dragged him towards the shore, near to which a boat, driven in by the tide, lay undulating; assisting him to enter, and to place Luxima within it, he put the only oar it contained into his hands; driving it from the shore, he himself returned to the scene of action.

The Missionary, wounded in his right arm, with difficulty managed the little bark; yet he instinctively plied the oar, and put out from the land, without any particular object in the effort—his thoughts were wild, his feelings were tumultuous—he was stunned, he was bewildered by the nature and rapidity of the events which had occurred. He saw the receding shore covered with smoke; he saw the flames ascending to Heaven, which were to have consumed him; he heard the discharge of firearms, and the shouts of horror and destruction: but the ocean was calm; the horizon was bathed in hues of living light, and the horrors he had escaped, gradually faded into distance, and sunk into silence. He steered the boat towards the rocky peninsula which is crowned by the fortress of Alguarda; he saw the crimson flag of the Inquisition hoisted from its ramparts—he saw a party of soldiers descending the rocks to gain a watch-tower, placed at the extremity of the peninsula, which guards the mouth of the bay:—here, remote as was the place, there was for him no asylum, no safety; he changed his course, and put out again to sea—twilight was deepening the shadows of evening; his little bark was no longer discernible from the land; he threw down the oar, he raised Luxima in his arms—her eye met his—she smiled languidly on him—he held her to his heart, and life and death were alike forgotten—but Luxima returned not the pressure of his embrace, she had swooned; and as he threw back her tresses, to permit the air to visit her face more freely, he perceived that they were *steeped in blood*! He now first discovered that the poignard he had escaped, had been received in the bosom of the Indian: distracted, he endeavoured to bind the wound with the scapular which had made a part of his death dress; but though he thus stopped for the time the effusion of blood, he could not recall her senses. He looked round him wildly, but there was no prospect of relief; he seized her in his arms, and turned his eyes on the deep, resolved to seek with her eternal repose in its bosom—he approached the edge of the boat—"To what purpose," he said, "do I struggle to protract, for a few hours, a miserable existence? Death we cannot escape, whatever way we turn—its horrors we may—O God! am I then obliged to add to the sum of my frailties and my sins the crimes of suicide and murder?" He gazed passionately on Luxima, and added, "Destroy thee, my beloved! while yet I feel the vital throb of that heart which has so long beaten only for me—oh, no! The Providence which has hitherto miraculously preserved us, may still make us the object of its care."—He laid Luxima gently down in the boat, and, looking round him, perceived that the moon, which was now rising, threw its light on a peninsula of rocks, which projected from the main land to a considerable distance into the sea—it was the light of heaven that guided him—he seized the oar, and plying it with all the strength he could yet collect, he soon reached the rocks, and perceived a cavern that seemed to open to receive and shelter them.

* * * * *

The Pundit of Lahore was among the few who escaped from the destruction he had himself excited. Pursued by a Spanish soldier, he had fled towards the shore, and, acquainted with all the windings of the rocks, their deep recesses and defiles, he had eluded the vigilance of the Spaniard, and reached a cavern, which held out a prospect of temporary safety, till his strength should be sufficiently recruited to permit him to continue his flight towards a port, where some Bengal vessels were stationed, which might afford him concealment, and convey him to a distant part of India: as he approached the cavern, he looked round it cautiously, and by the light of the moon, with which it was illuminated, he perceived that it was already occupied—for kneeling on the earth, the *Apostolic Nuncio* of India, supported on his bosom the dying *Priestess of Cashmire*. The Pundit rushed forward; "Fear not," he said, "be cheered, be comforted, all may yet go well: here we are safe for the present, and when we are able to proceed, some Bengalese merchantmen who lie at a little port at a short distance from hence, will give us conveyance to a settlement, where the power of Spain or of the Inquisition cannot reach us."

The presence, the words of the Pundit were balm to the harassed spirits of the Missionary; a faint hope beamed on his sinking heart, and he urged him to procure some fresh water among the rocks, the only refreshment for the suffering Indian, which the desolate and savage place afforded. The Pundit, having sought for a large shell to contain the water, flew in search of it; and the Missionary remained gazing upon Luxima, who lay motionless in his arms. The presence of the Pundit suddenly recalled to his memory the first scene of his mission; and he again beheld in fancy the youthful priestess of mystic love, borne triumphantly along amidst an idolizing multitude; he cast his eyes upon the object that lay faint and speechless in his arms; and the brilliant vision of his memory faded away, nor left upon his imagination one trace of its former lustre or its beauty; for the image which succeeded, was such as the *genius* of Despair could only pourtray in its darkest mood of gloomy creation.

In a rude and lonesome cavern, faintly lighted up by the rays of the moon, and echoing to the moaning murmurs of the ocean's tide, lay *that Luxima*, who once, like the delicious shade of her native region, seemed created only for bliss, and formed only for delight; those eyes, in whose glance the spirit of devotion, and the enthusiasm of tenderness, mingled their brilliancy and their softness, were now dim and beamless; and that bosom, where love lay enthroned beneath the vestal's veil, was stained with the lifeblood which issued from its almost exhausted veins. Motionless, and breathing with difficulty, and with pain, she lay in his arms, with no faculty but that of suffering, with no sensibility but that of pain:—he had found her like a remote and brilliant planet, shining in lone and distant glory, illuminating, by her rays, a sphere of harmony and peace; but she had for him deserted her *orbit*, and her light was now nearly extinguished for ever.

When the Pundit returned, he moistened her lips with water, and chafed her temples and her hands with the pungent herbs the surrounding rocks supplied; and when the vital hues of life again faintly revisited her cheek, the Missionary, as he gazed on the symptoms of returning existence, gave himself up to feelings of suspense and anxiety, to which despondency was almost preferable, and pressing those lips in death, which in life he would have deemed it the risk of salvation to touch, his soul almost mingled with that pure spirit, which seemed ready to escape with every low-drawn sigh; and his heart offered up its silent prayer to Heaven, that thus they might unite, and thus seek together mercy and forgiveness at its throne. *Luxima* revived, raised her eyes to those which were bent in agony and fondness over her, and on her look of suffering, and smile of sadness, beamed the ardour of a soul whose warm, tender, and imperishable feelings were still triumphant over even pain and death.

"Luxima!" exclaimed the Missionary, in a melancholy transport, and pressing her to a heart which a feeble hope cheered and re-animated, "*Luxima*, my beloved! wilt thou not struggle with death? wilt thou not save me from the horror of knowing, that it is *for me thou* diest? and that what remains of my wretched existence, has been purchased at the expence of thine? Oh! if *love*, which has led thee to death, can recall or attach thee to life, still live, even though thou livest *for my destruction*." A faint glow flushed the face of the Indian, her smile brightened, and she clung still closer to the bosom, whose throb now replied to the palpitation of her own.

"Yes," exclaimed the Missionary, answering the eloquence of her languid and tender looks, "yes, dearest, and most unfortunate, our destinies are now inseparably united! Together we have loved, together we have resisted, together we have erred, and together we have suffered; lost alike to the glory and the fame, which our virtues, and the conquest of our passions, once obtained for us; alike condemned by our religions and our countries, there now remains nothing on *earth* for us, but each other!—Already have we met the horrors of death, without its repose; and the life for which thou hast offered the precious purchase of thine own, must *now belong alone to thee*."

Luxima raised herself in his arms, and grasping his hands, and fixing on him her languid eyes, she articulated in a deep and tremulous voice, "*Father!*" but, faint from bodily exhaustion and mental emotion, she again sunk in silence on his bosom! At the plaintive sound of this touching and well-remembered epithet, the Missionary shuddered, and the blood froze round his sinking heart; again he heard the voice of the proselyte, as in the shades of Cashmire he had once heard it, when pure, and free from the taint of human frailty, he had addressed her only in the spiritual language of an holy mission, and she had heard him with a soul ignorant of human passion, and opening to receive that sacred truth, to whose cause he had proved so faithless: the religion he had offended, the zeal he had abandoned, the principles, the habits of feeling, and of thinking, he had relinquished, all rushed in this awful moment on his mind, and tore his conscience with penitence, and with remorse; he saw before his eyes the retribution of his error in the sufferings of its innocent cause; he sought to redeem what was yet redeemable of his fault, to recall to his wandering soul the duties of the minister of Heaven, and to put from his guilty thoughts the feelings of the impassioned man! He sought to withdraw his attention from the perishable woman, and to direct his efforts to the salvation of the immortal spirit; but when again he turned his eyes on the Indian, he perceived that hers were ardently fixed on the rosary of her idolatrous creed, to which she pressed with devotion her cold and quivering lips, while the crucifix which lay on her bosom was steeped in the blood she had shed to preserve him.

This affecting combination of images so opposite and so eloquent in their singular but natural association, struck on his heart with a force which his reason and his zeal had no power to resist:—and the words which religion, awakened to its duty, sent to his lips, died away in sounds inarticulate, from the mingled emotions of horror and compassion, of gratitude and love—and, wringing his hands, while cold drops hung upon his brow, he exclaimed in a tone of deep and passionate affliction, "Luxima, Luxima! are we then to be *eternally disunited*?"

Luxima replied only by a look of love, whose fond expression was the next moment lost in the convulsive distortions of pain. Much enfeebled by the sudden pang, a faintness, which resembled the sad torpor of death, hung upon her frame and features; yet her eyes were still fixed with a gaze so motionless and ardent, on the sole object of her dying thought, that her look seemed the last look of life and love, when both inseparably united dissolve and expire together. "Luxima," exclaimed the Missionary wildly, "Luxima, thou wilt not die! Thou wilt not leave me alone on earth to bear thy innocent blood upon my head, and thy insupportable loss for ever in my heart!—to wear out life in shame and desolation—my hope entombed with thee—my sorrows lonely and unparticipated—my misery keen and eternal!—Oh! no, fatal creature! sole cause of all I have ever known of bliss or suffering, of happiness or of despair, thou hast bound me to thee by dreadful ties; by bonds, sealed with thy blood, indissoluble and everlasting! And if thy hour is come, mine also is arrived, for triumphing over the fate which would divide us; we shall *die*, as we dared *not live*—together!"

Exhausted by the force and vehemence of an emotion which had now reached its crisis—enervated by tenderness, subdued by grief, and equally vanquished by bodily anguish, and by the still surviving conflicts of feeling and opinion—he sunk overpowered on the earth; and Luxima, held up by the sympathizing Pundit, seemed to acquire force from the weakness of her unfortunate friend, and to return from the grasp of death, that she might restore him to life. Endeavouring to support his head in her feeble arms, and pressing her cold cheek to his, she sought to raise and cheer his subdued spirit, by words of hope and consolation. At the sound of her plaintive voice, at the pressure of her soft cheek, the creeping blood quickened its circulation in his veins, and a faint sensation of pleasure thrilled on his exhausted nerves; he raised his head, and fixed his eyes on her face with one of those looks of passionate fondness, tempered by fear, and darkened by remorse, with which he had so frequently, in happier days, contemplated that exquisite loveliness which had first stolen between him and Heaven. Luxima still too well understood that look, which had so often given birth to emotions, which even approaching death had not quite annihilated; and with renovated strength (the illusory herald of dissolution) she exclaimed—"Soul of my life! the God whom thou adorest, did doubtless save thee from a dreadful death, that thou mightest live for others, and still he commands thee to bear the painful burthen of existence: yet, oh! if for others thou *wilt not live*, live at least for *Luxima!* and be thy beneficence to her nation, the redemption of those faults of which for thy sake she has been guilty!—Thy brethren will not dare to take a life, which God himself has miraculously preserved—and when *I* am no more, thou shalt preach, not to the Brahmins only, but to the Christians, that the sword of destruction, which has been this day raised between the followers of thy faith and of mine, may be for ever sheathed! Thou wilt appear among them as a spirit of peace, teaching mercy, and inspiring love; thou wilt soothe away, by acts of tenderness, and words of kindness, the stubborn prejudice which separates the mild and patient Hindu from his species; and thou wilt check the Christian's zeal, and bid him follow the sacred lesson of the God he serves, who, for years beyond the Christian era, has extended his merciful indulgence to the errors of the Hindu's mind, and bounteously lavished on his native soil those wondrous blessings which first tempted the Christians to seek our happier regions. But should thy eloquence and thy example fail, tell them my story! tell them how I have suffered, and how even thou hast failed:—thou, for whom I forfeited my cast, my country, and my life; for 'tis too true, that still *more loving* than enlightened, my ancient habits of belief clung to my mind, thou to my *heart*: still I lived thy seeming proselyte, that I might *still live thine*; and now *I die* as Brahmin women *die*, a *Hindu* in my feelings and my faith—dying for him I loved, and believing as my fathers have believed."

Exhausted and faint, she drooped her head on her bosom—and the Missionary, stiffened with horror, his human and religious feelings alike torn and wounded, hung over her, motionless and silent. The Pundit, dropping tears of compassion on the chilling hands he chafed, now administered some water to the parched lips of the dying Indian, on whose brow, the light of the moon shone resplendently. Somewhat revived by the refreshment, she turned on him her languid but grateful eyes, and slowly recognizing his person, a faint blush, like the first doubtful colouring of the dawn, suffused the paleness of her cheek; she continued to gaze earnestly on him for some moments, and a few tears, the last she ever shed, fell from her closing eyes,—and though the springs of life were nearly exhausted, yet her fading spirits rallied to the recollection of *home!* of *friends!* of *kindred!* and of *country!* which the presence of a sympathizing compatriot thus painfully and tenderly awakened—then, after a convulsive struggle between life and death, whose shadows were gathering on her countenance, she said in a voice scarcely audible, and in great emotion—"I owe thee much, let me owe thee more—thou seest before thee Luxima! the Prophetess and Brachmachira of Cashmire!—and thou wast haply sent by the interposition of Providence to receive her last words, and to be the testimony to her people of her innocence; and when thou shalt return to the blessed paradise of her nativity, thou wilt say—'that having gathered *a dark spotted flower in the garden of love*, she expiates her error by the loss of her life; that her disobedience to the forms of her religion and the laws of her country, was punished by days of suffering, and by an untimely death; yet that her *soul* was pure from sin, as, when clothed in transcendent brightness, she outshone, in faith, in *virtue*, all women of her nation!' "

This remembrance of her former glory, deepened the hues of her complexion, and illumined a transient ray of triumph in her almost beamless eyes: then pausing for a moment, she fixed her glance on the image of her tutelar god, which she still held in her hand—the idol, wearing the form of infant beauty, was symbolic of that religious mystic love, to which she had *once* devoted herself! she held it for a moment to her lips, and to her heart—then, presenting it to the Cashmirian, she added, "Take it, and bear it back to him, from whom I received it, on the day of my consecration, in the *temple of Serinagur!* to him! the aged grandsire whom I abandoned!—dear and venerable!—should he still survive the loss and shame of her, his child and his disciple! should he still deign to acknowledge as *his* offspring the outcast whom he cursed—the Chancalas whom—" the words died away upon her quivering lips, "Brahma!" she faintly exclaimed, "Brahma!" and, grasping the hands of the Missionary, alternately directed her looks to him and to Heaven; but he replied not to the last glance of life and love. He had sunk beneath the acuteness of his feelings; and the Indian, believing that his spirit had fled before her own to the realms of eternal peace, and there awaited to receive her, bowed her head, and expired in the blissful illusion, with a smile of love and a ray of religious joy shedding their mingled lustre on her slowly closing eyes.

* * * * *

* * * * *

The guards, who by order of the Inquisition were sent in pursuit of the fugitives, reached the cavern of their retreat three days after that of the insurrection; but here they found only a pile partly consumed, and the ashes of such aromatic plants as the interstices of the surrounding rocks afforded, which the Hindus usually burn with the bodies of their deceased friends, at the funeral pyre; they continued therefore their search farther along the shore; it was long, persevering and fruitless. The Apostolic Nuncio of India was *never heard of more*.

Time rolled on, and the majestic order of nature, uninterrupted in its harmonious course, finely contrasted the rapid vicissitudes of human events, and the countless changes in human institutions! In the short space of *twenty* years, the mighty had fallen, and the lowly were elevated; the lash of oppression had passed alternately from the grasp of the persecutor to the hand of the persecuted; the slave had seized the sceptre, and the tyrant had submitted to the chain. Portugal, resuming her independence, carried the standard of her triumph even to the remote shores of the Indian ocean, and, knowing no ally but that of *compatriot unanimity*, resisted by her single and unassisted force, the combined powers of a mighty state, the intrigues of a wily cabinet, and the arms of a successful potentate.[19] While *Freedom* thus

[19] Revolution of Portugal.

unfurled her spotless banner in a remote corner of the West, she lay mangled and in chains, at the foot of victorious tyranny in the East. *Aurengzebe* had waded through carnage and destruction to the throne of India—he had seized a sceptre stained with a brother's blood, and wore the diadem, torn from a parent's brow! worthy to represent the most powerful and despotic dynasty of the earth, his genius and his fortunes resembled the regions he governed, mingling sublimity with destruction; splendour with peril;—and combining, in their mighty scale, the great extremes of good and evil. Led by a love of pleasure, or allured by a natural curiosity, he resolved on visiting the most remote and most delicious province of his empire, where his ancestors had so often sought repose from the toils of war, and fatigue of government; and where, *twenty years* before, his own heroic and unfortunate nephew, Solymon Sheko, had sought asylum and resource against his growing power and fatal influence. He left *Delhi* for Cashmire, during an interval of general prosperity and peace, and performed his expedition with all the pomp of eastern magnificence.[20]

In the immense and motley multitude which composed his suite, there was an European *Philosopher*, who, highly distinguished by the countenance and protection of the emperor, had been led, by philosophical curiosity and tasteful research, to visit a country, which, more celebrated than known, had not yet attracted the observation of genius, or the inquiry of science. He found the natural beauty of the vale of *Cashmire*, far exceeding the description of its scenes which lived in the songs of the Indian bards, and its mineral and botanic productions curious, and worthy of the admiration and notice of the naturalist; and in a spot which might be deemed the region of natural phenomena, he discovered more than *one* object to which a moral interest was attached. Yet to *one object only* did the *interest of sentiment* peculiarly belong; it was a sparry cavern, among the hills of Serinagur, called, by the *natives* of the valley, the "*Grotto of congelations*!"[21] They pointed it out to strangers as a place constructed by magic, which for many years had been the residence of a recluse! a stranger, who had appeared suddenly among

[20] Historical.

[21] Monsieur de Bernier laments, in his interesting account of his journey to Cashmire which he performed in the suite of Aurengzebe, that circumstances prevented him visiting the grotto of congelations, of which so many strange tales were related by the natives of the valley.

them, who had been rarely seen, and more rarely addressed, who led a lonely and an innocent life, equally avoided and avoiding, who lived unmolested, awakening no interest, and exciting no persecution—"he was," they said, "a wild and melancholy man! whose religion was unknown, but who prayed at the confluence of rivers, at the rising and the setting of the sun; living on the produce of the soil, he needed no assistance, nor sought any intercourse; and his life, thus slowly wearing away, gradually faded into death."

A *goalo*, or Indian shepherd, who missed him for several mornings at his wonted place of matinal devotion, was led by curiosity or by compassion to visit his grotto. He found him dead, at the foot of an altar which he had himself raised to the deity of his secret worship, and fixed in the attitude of one who died in the act of prayer. Beside him lay a small urn, formed of the sparry congelations of the grotto—on opening it, it was only found to contain some ashes, a cross stained with blood, and the dsandum of an Indian Brahmin. On the lucid surface of the *urn* were carved some characters which formed the name of "*Luxima!*"—It was the name of an *outcast*, and had long been condemned to oblivion by the crime of its owner. The Indians shuddered when they pronounced it! and it was believed that the *Recluse* who lived so long and so unknown among them, was the same, who once, and in days long passed, had seduced, from the altar of the god she served, the most celebrated of their religious women, when he had visited their remote and lovely valley in the character of

A Christian Missionary.

THE END.

9 789361 381331

Printed by Libri Plureos GmbH in Hamburg,
Germany